Bound Treasure

Masters of the Prairie Winds Club
Book Four

by Avery Gale

Dedication

A special thanks to Cathy Bryant for reminding me that some people are real treasures...rather, they are the kind that need to be buried at the bottom of the sea. The conversation was not about the book I was writing...but it inspired the title...a detail I'd been struggling with. Cathy's sense of humor sees me through each and every time I think I've hit the wall...and I thank her for always listening, gently prodding me in the right direction, and consistently adding sparkle to my life.

Prologue

Ten years ago

"REGINA—LET ME HELP you…come on, get out of your gear quickly. You have to hide. I don't know who is coming, but we aren't expecting anyone and I'm worried the family has found us." Her father's voice was frantic and his gaze kept flickering to the speedboats that were quickly closing in off the starboard quarter of their boat. She'd just come back onboard after helping him document the site of his latest discovery. As always, their boat was anchored a substantial distance from the actual wreckage in an effort to keep pirates from knowing the exact location of their find. They had already stored the smaller boat they used to travel to the site back in its hidden storage area along the port side. She heard her mother shout something to her father about taking "it" to their stateroom, but Regina wasn't sure what she was referring to.

Peeling off her wetsuit, she'd barely had time to pull a t-shirt over her head before her dad removed the gold chain and Hunab Ku symbol he always wore and slipped it over her head. He dropped the heavy gold pendant inside her shirt, then leaned forward to press a kiss to her damp forehead before shoving her toward the small closet along the main deck. He'd known how frightened she was of small, dark spaces and she was grateful he'd chosen one of the hiding places they'd designed for her that had a lou-vered door that let in enough light to keep her panic at bay. He lifted her to the top shelf and shoved her to the very back before packing old, foul smelling gear in front of her. At first Regina wasn't sure she'd be able to keep from gagging, but she knew this wasn't the time to argue with him.

"I want you to stay quiet. No matter what happens, you are not to make any sound whatsoever, do you understand? Do not come out until your mama or I come to get you. If we can't for some reason, you stay hidden until you know everyone is gone and then you shimmy out the trap door behind you. Make sure you turn on the locator beacon before you call for help. Do you remember how to run the radio?" At her nod he continued, "If we get separated, remember Hunab Ku will give you everything your heart most desires if you will just follow its path. Never let it out of your hands. If you have to leave the boat, take the one thing that holds your heart's desire. Promise me you won't forget and that you will stay perfectly quiet, sweetheart."

"I promise, Papa."

"One more thing…your mother and I love you with everything we are. And we are very proud of the young woman you are becoming. Remember…follow your heart, it will lead you to unimaginable treasures." With that, he closed the door and the darkness seemed to swallow her whole. She shifted just enough that her eyes could see between the smelly tarps and nets through the slats of the door. While her narrowed view of the deck helped ease her claustrophobia, it also proved to be one of the most devastating decisions of her life.

Chapter One

REGI STARED DOWN in horror at the newspaper spread out before her. The story about the unusual wedding of two drop-dead gorgeous retired Navy SEALs marrying the same woman would have been big news any day, but when you took into account they were the sons of self-made billionaires Steve and Susie McCall, it was tabloid heaven. Every rag reporter in North America would be clamoring for an angle on the story and flying below the radar was going to be virtually impossible.

There wasn't just one photograph there were three…three that clearly showed her face. Regi's hope the make-up artist the grooms' mother had hired had made her unrecognizable, it vanished the instant she'd opened the paper and looked down to see her mother's face staring back at her. She'd always been told she looked like her dad, but with her hair fixed and make-up on, there was no doubt her mother had left her genetic mark as well. How had she not recognized that particular problem when she'd looked in the mirror before the ceremony? Trying to steady her breathing wasn't working and Regi could feel her control beginning to slip. Crap on a cottontail, anyone who knew her mother was going to know instantly where the missing Stephano daughter was now.

Regi had been worried there might be a picture of her on some back page blip, but even in her worst nightmares she hadn't imagined this. Knowing the worst was yet to come sent her heart rate into launch mode. The Austin Chronicle's double page spread was sure to be picked up by national news outlets and from there it would be world-wide news within minutes. Knowing it was only a matter of hours before the pictures were in the hands of every thug with a gun wanting to make a name for himself with "the family", was enough to make her dizzy. Regi dropped into her chair behind the reception desk in the Prairie Winds Club's elegant entrance and put her head between her knees.

Taking deep breaths hoping to banish the black dots that had begun dancing in her vision, Regi squeezed her eyes shut trying to focus on her brain's need for oxygen rather than the pictures she'd just seen. How had the photographer managed to snap so many shots of her without her knowledge? *Might have been the fact you were too focused on the Masters of Menace instead of paying attention. Maybe you should have been thinking with your head instead of letting your girly parts rule the night. Great, now I'm carrying on conversations with myself, next thing you know I'll be spewing it aloud like Tobi. I swear she is contagious.*

A snort of laughter pulled Regi out of her thoughts, when her eyes flew open she wanted to groan. Didn't it just figure the first thing she'd see would be black boots she knew belonged to Dr. Kirk Evans. Black and gently scuffed, the boots that were mere inches from her face obviously belonged to a man who was comfortable wearing them. These weren't "city-boy boots" that hadn't ever even seen a cow. No, these boots belonged to a man who had been raised wearing them, a man who was as comfortable in the saddle as he was seeing patients in his upscale medical clinic.

Oh yeah, these boots belonged to a man who could turn her body every which way but loose with just a few words…and had done exactly that on more than one occasion. And right now, the caress of calloused fingers along the back of her neck reminded her just how familiar those hands were with her body. When she tried to sit up, his gentle grip held her in place and warm breath brushed over her ear as he spoke softly, "No, *muñeca*, stay where you are for a moment." Regi didn't want to obey him, but the submissive in her reacted to his Master's voice before her brain could object to being called a doll.

"Breathe with me." His words were warm against the shell of her ear and even though she couldn't see him, the gentle brush of his breath moving over the side of her face brought her breathing in sync with his. He didn't rush her and the soft stroking of his fingers over the back of her neck was so soothing it was erotic. When she heard other voices murmuring in the background Regi stiffened and tried once again to sit up but Kirk's firm grasp held her in place. "No, *guapa*. Stay where you are for a bit. The only person you should be concerned with has his lips pressed against your ear." As much as Regi liked the sound of his Spanish endearments, she knew full well she wasn't gorgeous, but she wasn't really in a position to argue the point at the moment. *Nope, head between knees to keep from crashing to the floor pretty much negates my position of power to debate anything. Damn and double damn.*

Regi knew what it was like to tumble over the edge into panic, it had happened all too frequently during those first few years after her parents had died. Now she found herself clinging to his voice as if it were a lifeline thrown to her just before going under for the last time. A part of her knew she was making a mistake, but the larger part was responding to the words of a man she trusted even when she didn't want to. Kirk Evans knew exactly how to gain her compliance and right now, he was using every bit of that knowledge. His skilled fingers drew slow circles at the base of her skull easing the tension as the memories of all the ways those same fingers had lit up her world a couple of nights earlier began flashing through her mind sending a rush of sexual heat and desperate need straight to her sex. "I can smell your arousal, *mi amõre*. And I have to say, I enjoy it much more than your fear."

Oh fuck a bunny, could this possibly get any more embarrassing? Maybe I should just give in? After all, what difference will it make if I've had wild monkey sex with the wack-a-doodle doctor duo when some asshat with a gun shows up at my door? At least I'll die happy, right? There has to be some special place in the cracker factory for people who have entire conversations with themselves…and somebody should reserve me a room.

KIRK EVANS HAD been on his way out the front door of the Prairie Winds Club after stopping in to visit two of his favorite patients. He'd met with Tobi West and Gracie McDonald in the gazebo behind the club to discuss plans for their upcoming deliveries before their four husbands had joined them. As usual, the women were full of piss and vinegar as his mom would say, and Kirk had enjoyed his time with them. Watching the interaction between his friends and their women was always entertaining. It also fed his hope that he and his best friend and business partner, fellow OB-GYN, Brian Bennett, would be able to build a similar relationship with the right woman.

They had long discussed the possibility of sharing a

woman. Because their patients rarely decided to give birth during traditional office hours one of them was always on call and sharing a woman made sense when more often than not they were called back to the hospital for hours on end. On the rare occasions they'd pursued women as individuals, their time with her was so fractured they had never been able to form the deep bonds of trust and feelings of security a true submissive needs to flourish in a Dominant/submissive relationship.

When they'd met Regina Turner, both he and Brian had known she was perfect for them. There was a soul-deep fire burning in the tiny woman that was impossible for either of them to turn away from. And despite the fact she was still fighting their mutual attraction as if her life depended on it, there was little doubt in anyone's mind that she craved what they had to offer but was too frightened to reach out and grab it. When she'd agreed to let them escort her to her friend Jen's wedding they'd been sure things were headed in the right direction. The evening had gone perfectly once they'd gotten her to relax. Smiling to himself, he remembered just how effectively two flutes of champagne had melted away her outer shields. The wild monkey sex they'd shared had given them the opportunity to crash through several more layers of those glass blocks she'd built around herself.

The next morning, Regi had seemed pensive when they'd mentioned the rumor they'd heard about her moving. She hadn't acted as if she was being secretive, it had seemed more like embarrassment about being forced to move from her small basement apartment. Micah Drake had told them what he'd overheard and had also mentioned the Wests had offered her one of the small cottages behind Prairie Winds. Kirk had made some inquiries around town and discovered the old home she lived in had recently been condemned. The building slated to be razed by the local historical society. Kirk had shaken his head and wondered what condition her small apartment was in, but considering the outrageous amount she'd been paying in rent—hell, he probably didn't really want to know.

He and Brian had been watching her carefully after Jax and Micah mentioned their concerns about Regi's emotional state several months ago. Brian had made a late night house call to check on Gracie early in her pregnancy. After their wife was finally settled, the two men had brought up their concerns about the club's vivacious business manager. Kirk had been at the hospital that night, so Brian had gone over to treat the overwhelming morning sickness Gracie had experienced early in her pregnancy. They didn't see cases as extreme as hers very often and they'd teased her husbands they might have trouble convincing her to have a second child. As badly as he'd felt for Gracie, he'd also been grateful Brian had gotten the opportunity to speak with Jax and Micah. Their heads-up had come at a critical time because he and Brian had been getting close to giving up hope that Regi might be "the one".

Micah hadn't shared everything he knew about Regi, but he'd given them enough to know her issues weren't particularly with either of them, but were related to some horrific trauma she had witnessed as a teen. When Kirk had pressed Brian for more information, he'd said the only other thing Micah had told him was that he wished Regi would judge herself based on her brave actions after the fact rather than the incident itself. The entire conversation had seemed stilted to Kirk, but then he had always been much more direct. If you wanted *tact* you needed to talk to Brian, but if you wanted to hear it *straight up*, then Kirk was your man.

Today, he'd been focused on moving through the club's large entry and had almost missed her. If she hadn't been talking to herself, he wouldn't have noticed her behind the chest high counter. Stepping around the desk, he'd been worried when he saw Regi sitting with her head between her knees. Her entire body was shuddering and he knew she was trying desperately to keep from passing out. He had also known the instant she became aware of his presence because he hadn't been able to hold back his chuckle when she'd said that Tobi West was contagious. Several Doms in the club who would agree with her. The club owners' sweet wife was as submissive as they came, but she was also smart, opinionated, and ornery enough to challenge a saint.

Kirk had been pleased when Regi settled back down at his touch. He wasn't sure exactly what had triggered her panicked response, but he was willing to bet it had something to do with the pictures of her displayed so prominently in the newspaper spread over her desk. He'd knelt down and kept speaking softly against the side of her face, letting the warmth of his breath move over her clammy skin as he thumbed open his phone and sent a quick text to Kyle West. Before he'd finally let her sit back up, both Kyle and his twin, Kent, had come into the room. They were followed shortly by Micah Drake and Jax McDonald. Kirk had smiled at the way the four former SEALs had managed to make it to Regi's side so quickly and without making so much as a whisper of sound.

When Kyle quirked a brow at him with questions in his eyes, Kirk merely nodded to the newspaper. All four men blanched when they saw the pictures and Kirk resolved right then to press for answers. He didn't plan to be as accepting of the lame explanation Micah had given Brian. Rocking forward, he pressed a soft kiss against Regi's cheek. "How are you doing, *muñeca?*" On any other day, referring to her as a "doll" would have sent a dark cloud racing through her expression, but today it was obviously the least of her concerns. Her stuttered breath let him know she was still trying to settle herself but she'd had her head down long enough and he was beginning to worry about how unsteady she was going to be when she sat up again. "Come on, let me help you. We're going to Kent and Kyle's office so we can find out what this is about." He didn't wait for her to respond, he just slid his arms under her knees and around her back and lifted her effortlessly into the cradle of his arms. Regi was petite by anyone's standards and carrying her pressed against his chest seemed to settle them both. She was barely five foot tall with a delicate bone structure that made her look like a pixie. But her long flowing auburn hair had always reminded him of *The Little Mermaid*…Ariel, but he'd certainly never tell her as much.

Regi had cuddled against him like a kitten and for just a moment he wished he hadn't alerted the others to the problem. He heard the crinkle of the newspaper and knew one of them was bringing it as they followed him down the hall. Kyle stepped around him and opened the door, the concern Kirk saw in his friend's face made him grateful Regi worked for people who obviously cared a great deal about her.

Kirk moved across the spacious room and sat on the large sofa. He settled the warm bundle of woman in his arms onto his lap and tipped her chin up until her eyes met his. "Would you like something to drink, Regi?" Kent was already opening a bottle of water and handing it to him before she'd even answered. "Here, take a couple of drinks of this before we talk." When she'd finished Kirk saw the apprehension in her eyes. She might have known they weren't alone, but he doubted she'd known how many people had joined them. Kirk saw Jax hold up his phone in question, and giving a quick nod, he watched the man step from the room knowing he was placing a call to Brian. As much as Kirk would like his friend to be there for the entire conversation, this was a discussion that wasn't going to wait.

He and Brian had spent hundreds of hours discussing the type of relationship they envisioned with the woman they'd claim as their own. One of the "givens" in their lives was the fact a great deal of the time one or the other of them would be working, so the other would be dealing with their wife individually. They'd had years to discuss a thousand different scenarios and had rarely disagreed about how a situation should be handled. Even though Kirk was confident he was handling the situation exactly as Brian would, he appreciated Jax's offer to make the call. Brian deserved the chance to hear as much of the coming discussion as possible because Kirk's gut told him it was a complicated story.

Chapter Two

REGI WANTED NOTHING more than to stay cuddled against Kirk's warmth with her eyes closed, shutting out the rest of the world for a little longer, but she knew it wouldn't work. If there was one thing she had learned while working for the Wests' ultra-exclusive fetish club, it was that Doms weren't keen on letting a submissive hide— it didn't matter who or what the sub was hiding from— they called them out...period. And even though she hadn't actually seen anyone else yet, she'd definitely picked up the scents of a couple of different men so she didn't hold out much hope for beating a fast retreat.

Finally relenting, Regi looked around the room and wished she hadn't. She saw both of her bosses and Micah Drake. She'd heard the door latch a moment earlier so she knew someone else had been in the room as well. Knowing the men as well as she did, her money was on Jax McDonald exiting the room to call Brian Bennett, but only time would tell. It didn't seem likely she'd be lucky enough that Tobi or Gracie would make an appearance, but she could always hope. Both women were nearing the end of their pregnancy and spent so much time resting, Regi worried they'd mold if she didn't roll them over often enough.

Realizing she was sitting on Kirk's lap in front of the other Doms was unnerving and Regi hadn't even started to move when his arms tightened around her. "Stop. Stay right where you are. I like having you close and I'll be able to monitor your condition much better this way."

How does he do that? How did he know I was going to move? Regi might not be the most experienced submissive in the club, but she wasn't a newbie either, and even she knew his words had been code for 'I'll be able to tell if you are lying.'

Every Dom Regi knew shamelessly used his or her submissive's responses as their own personal polygraph, and the worst part was they were rarely wrong in their interpretations. Of course, she'd always thought the tactic was more than just a little unfair; after all, how could anyone hope to keep their social mask in place when they were being battered by the storm of sexual stimulation that made everything but their Dom's touch fade into a foggy haze?

Dominants at Prairie Winds were either experienced or they were mentored by one of the club's Masters until the owners felt they were ready to be entrusted with a submissive's safety. Masters and Dungeon Monitors were the best and most experienced Dominants among the members and every man in the room with her was the cream of that very elite group. *Yes indeed…if you dreamt up a pot of pickle soup to fall into you couldn't have done any better than this, Regina Sue.*

Deciding this wasn't going to be one of those "the best defense is a good offense" moments, Regi sat quietly and waited. The silence was beginning to become uncomfortable and she wasn't entirely certain what they were waiting for until Jax walked back in with Peter following close on his heels. Regi didn't know much about Peter Weston other than he was one of the newest members of the team the Wests were putting together. But the Prairie Wind's rumor mill was functioning at gale force with regard to the fact the man seemed to respond to exactly what a sub was thinking. She'd heard him described as everything from a gifted empath to just plain spooky. And the fact Jax McDonald had decided to include him in this discussion was more than a bit unnerving. *Just what I need. As if four Doms in the room isn't going to be tough enough, they have to bring in a stranger who can read minds? This job is getting to be a really big pain in my ass. First those fucking pictures and now this…hell, this will probably make the Spanish Inquisition look like a Sesame Street playdate.* Regi didn't know how long she'd been lost in her own thoughts until she realized her eyes had been locked on her tightly clenched fists and her fingers were numb from the effort. Looking up, the first thing she noticed was how deathly still the room seemed. The men surrounding her looked like statues, with the notable exception of Peter Weston, who was gazing at her intently, a knowing smile gracing his full lips. *Well, frack!*

PETER HAD JUST walked in the back door of the club when his phone vibrated against his hip. Keeping the ringer off had become such habit while he'd been a part of the Teams he still wasn't comfortable with the sound of it ringing when he was working. He smiled as he considered the fact he hadn't really retired from Special Forces work, he'd merely traded one employer for another. He was technically still a member of a Black Ops team, but this time he was working for Kyle and Kent West rather than directly for Uncle Sam. He hoped the position he'd accepted would make his transition to civilian life easier.

His best friend appeared to have seamlessly traded one job for another with his usual laissez faire attitude, but Peter knew Carl Phillips almost as well as he knew himself and saw the turbulence brewing below the surface. It would take a while for the storm to break, but when it did, it was a wild ride until Carl managed to steer himself into calmer waters. Shaking his head in an effort to refocus his attention on the trembling woman sitting on her Master's lap, he watched and listened. He wasn't sure how he felt about the number of people in the Wests' office. Peter had learned early in life not to tell people about his gift because most either discounted it or wanted to exploit it. However, being able to hear the thoughts of others wasn't a secret easily kept when you were a Special Forces operative because it had often meant the difference between life and death. The bottom line was, he wouldn't keep a secret that had the potential to hurt someone else. Integrity always trumped personal convenience.

As always, stepping into an emotionally charged situation and opening up his mind was like walking face first into a wall of noise. He'd once described it to his team as standing in the middle of Best Buy with every device in the store playing something different while the store shifted beneath your feet like a cheap carnival ride. It wasn't a perfect description, but it was as close as he'd ever gotten. He moved closer to Regi so he could zero in on her and wasn't surprised that she'd noticed him enter the room, however, she'd zoned-out again, causing his sudden proximity to startle her a few moments later. What did surprise him was the whirl of emotions surrounding her. She was clearly upset about photos but it was her determination to face the problem alone that he knew was going to be the bigger issue they'd need to tackle.

When Regi looked up and locked gazes with him, Peter could tell she was thrown by the intensity of his regard. He'd managed to keep his expression impassive until she'd come up with the *Sesame Street* remark and then he hadn't been able to hold back his amusement at her sarcasm. Admittedly, he didn't know Regi well, but from the little he'd heard and seen, this was much more like her usual M.O. and he was relieved she was bouncing back from whatever had shaken her. He'd seen the knowledge light up her eyes when she'd realized he had *heard* her so there was no reason to hold back his comment. "Regi, while I'm amused by the *Sesame Street* reference because I have watched my fair share of those shows with my brother's rambunctious troop of yard apes, I can assure you this group is much more devious than those lame bastards responsible for the Spanish Inquisition."

Peter gave her a few seconds to process what he'd said and comprehend the deeper meaning of his words before continuing. One of the first things he'd picked up as a kid who could hear what others were thinking and feel their emotions was the fact the single biggest mistake people make when talking to others was their habit of blundering ahead without giving the other person a chance to process what they'd said. He'd found that waiting until whatever words he had spoken stopped bouncing around in the other person's mind improved communication exponentially.

Kyle had approached him right after he'd arrived at Prairie Winds about collaborating with Jen McCall to teach a communications class for club staff and the team of operatives they were assembling. Jen's expertise in body language and linguistics combined with the techniques he'd learned for improving understanding would put their operatives ahead of the game in hostage rescues and any role a team member might assume when undercover. Since Kyle had already scheduled their first meeting for the day after Jen, Sage, and Sam returned from their honeymoon, Peter was sure his new bosses were serious about preparing their teams in every way possible. When he'd finally heard Regi's mind settle, Peter sat down on a chair facing Regi and simply said, "Talk to me, Regi."

Peter knew Brian Bennett had slipped into the back door of the Wests' office because he could literally feel the apprehension vibrating off the man. He was fairly certain Regi hadn't heard him come into the room and he wondered what effect the other doc's presence would have and was surprised how quickly that question was answered.

"WHAT WOULD YOU like to talk about, Peter? Are there scheduling conflicts that need to be checked? Or perhaps a payroll issue? I just heard the back door snick shut so I assume someone called Dr. Bennett came in as well. Yes indeed, I must be ready for the cracker factory because hail, hail the gang's all here." Regi knew she was digging herself into a hole, but she wasn't going to hand over the information they wanted that damned easily.

Do they really think it's going to be that simple? That I'll just blurt out the whole story? Paint a picture of the horror I saw play out on the deck that day? Dredge up all the grisly details so they can look at me differently from this point forward? Fuck me, I hope I don't look like that big of a pushover. And calling in another doctor is really just over the top.

Regi knew that every man in the room would see her differently when they learned what had happened. When the court appointed counselors had first mention the term "victim prejudice" to her, Regi had discounted the concept because it had seemed utterly ridiculous. But she had soon discovered it was all too real. Even the police in that little hut the closest officials called a police department had treated her differently after their interviews. Before they'd known exactly what she'd seen, they'd been polite, but all business. However, after she'd told them her story, their expressions had been filled with pity and she'd hated it. Being seen as a victim always made her feel weak, and she'd learned quickly to edit her answers. After she'd been turned over to U.S. officials, she'd been forced to tell the story so many times she'd started changing it just for her own entertainment. It hadn't been any big surprise to learn only one man had noticed. Charlie Hendricks had been the first man to board the boat after her frantic call for help and he'd stuck to her like glue. When she'd started playing with the investigators, he'd always leaned casually against a wall with his arms crossed over his chest and watched impassively. She'd seen him bite back a smile occasionally when she'd been particularly creative, but most of the time he just watched and listened.

Charlie was the only one that had not treated her as if she'd suddenly contracted the plague. He'd helped her navigate the legal system when the state had deemed it in her best interest to put her in her maternal grandmother's custody…the twisted irony of that had boggled Regi's imagination and left her with a deep distrust of all things "system" related. Charlie had been the one who managed to find a judge willing to declare her a legal adult despite the fact she had just turned sixteen. When it became clear the various federal agencies that had involved themselves in the case were going to spend the foreseeable future arguing about who was responsible for the granddaughter of one of the world's most notorious crime families, Charlie once again stepped in. He'd obtained funding to setup a small trust fund for her to use for educational purposes and altered her identity enough to let her live in relative safety. She'd moved to Texas, enrolled in college a month later, and never looked back. Regi kept in contact with Charlie and had offered to move to Florida when he'd found out he had terminal cancer, but he'd made her promise to stay put. She'd choked back her tears as she'd listened to him as he insisted the best thing she could do for him was stay safe. He'd told her during one of their late night phone calls that he was worried she was still "marked" because even after he had retired he'd fielded requests for information about her whereabouts.

Regi had never understood why she'd become such a target. It wasn't as if she was laying claim to any of *the family's* money. She had very little left that had belonged to her parents…a small wooden box that her mother had used for her favorite jewelry and pictures was the only thing Regi had managed to hide inside her coat the night she'd been rescued from the boat. The agents who had seemed to materialize from thin air hadn't wanted her to take anything…not even her own clothing and personal items, but she had finally managed to persuade them that her clothes and make-up weren't a threat to national security. When she'd gone into her parents stateroom to get a coat she'd seen the box and known she'd likely never get another chance to hold anything in her hand that had belonged to her mom, so she had stuffed the box inside the coat.

Walking off the boat that night, seeing dark blood stains discoloring the wooden deck was one of the most difficult things Regi ever had to do. A part of her had wanted to stay on that boat. What if those covered blood-stains weren't really from her mom and dad? Maybe they were still floating out in the warm waters off shore waiting to be rescued? What if all of it was some big mistake? They'd be really worried when they returned to find her missing. How would they ever be able to find her? A voice calling her name brought her back to the moment and she shook her head, scattering the memories she'd been lost in like dry leaves in the west Texas wind.

Chapter Three

PETER LISTENED INTENTLY as Regi's thoughts raced. He'd shaken his head vigorously when Brian Bennett had stepped forward. It had been obvious the good doc had planned to pull her back to the present when she'd started shaking and crying, but Peter had wanted to get as much as he could before she had a chance to rebuild the shields. He'd been completely blindsided by the images he'd seen go through her mind. He knew he'd gotten only a small portion of it, and even that little bit was disjointed, but her emotional response was what had been utterly devastating. When it became clear she was sliding over into a full-blown panic attack, he'd motioned for Brian to step in. "Call her name until you get a response. But don't shake her or you'll send her over. Right now she is caught between her memories and the present."

Scooting back, he watched as Kirk Evans continued rubbing soothing circles over her back and Brian enclosed her clenched fists in his hands. Seeing the seamless way the men worked as a team to pull Regi back from the edge was gratifying. They were both experienced sexual Dominants and had obviously worked together with subs for a long time because they easily anticipated each other's next move. Peter moved to the side to speak with the other men in the room giving them a brief run-down of what he'd learned. There wasn't any doubt the one agent who'd

helped her would be able to give them far more information. He reminded them that his gift was far from
infallible, but he really hoped he had been able to give
them enough to begin mapping out a strategy to keep her
safe. There wasn't much about the whole thing that made
sense and in his experience, this kind of confusion was
usually created for a reason.

ONCE REGI HAD settled back in the present, she'd stood
from Kirk's lap and moved to one of the wing-backed
chairs. They'd given her that distance because it was
obvious she needed it to pull herself back together. She sat
so rigid, Brian had wanted to smile at her perfect posture
knowing how much his mom was going to appreciate that
particular habit. His mom had bopped both he and his
sister upside their heads any time she'd found them
"slouching like a Walmart special". Hell, he still had great
posture to this day thanks to her obsession and ridiculously
long reach. This was the first time he'd pulled up a
memory of his sister without feeling like someone was
lancing his heart with a sword, and he didn't doubt for a
minute the petite wildflower in front of him was the
reason. Regi actually reminded him of Beth in many
ways...a personality that seemed disproportionately large
for her small frame, her tendency to use humor as a shield,
and her run-to-the-roar attitude that made her dangerously
reckless.

After she'd taken a few more drinks from the bottle of
water Kirk had handed to her earlier, she shocked them all
by methodically laying out everything that had happened
to her. Her voice was almost robot like. Her face and voice

were totally lacking in any affect and the even paced monotone she used when speaking was almost eerie in its detachment. Brian knew Kirk would also note the objective way she related the details of that afternoon made it seem as if she were narrating in third person rather than giving an eyewitness account. Every man in the room had some training related to working with victims of trauma, but Brian was certain they didn't have the experience he and Kirk had. When her words started slurring and the tiny trembles he'd first seen in her hands became full-blown quaking, Brian stepped forward and squatted down in front of her. Smoothing his fingers from her temple down over her cheek until his palm cupped the underside of her jaw effectively silencing her, he quietly said, "That's enough for now, baby."

How she'd managed to tell the entire story without shedding a single tear was a testament to her determination and strength, so when a single tear breached the dam of each eye to trickle slowly down her cheeks, Brian felt as if someone had kicked him squarely in the chest. Sliding an arm under her knees and behind her back, he lifted her easily. At six foot four, his height was often inconvenient, but it was a blessed advantage today as he quickly made his way down a short hall to the first aid station. Regi wasn't in need of medical care, but she was desperately in need of a little TLC.

KIRK WATCHED BRIAN carry Regi out of the room and noted the several moments of silence that filled the office. Leaning back in his chair, he took a deep breath and considered all she'd been through. There wasn't any way to fully understand how much of a toll an experience like that would take on someone, no matter how old they were. Hell, he didn't know many adults who would be able to cope with the emotional fallout of that kind of experience.

It wasn't a surprise to anyone that Kyle West was the first to speak. "After hearing her story, I am humbled beyond words at her strength. That being said, I also want to paddle her ass for not telling us sooner. We could have kept these pictures out of the paper had we known." His voice dropped and he added, "I wish I knew why the hell this club seems to be grand central for independent subs who are brilliant but sometimes don't appear to have a lick of common sense or even the barest comprehension of self-preservation." Kirk wanted to laugh because it seemed his last words were likely spoken more to himself than anyone else in the room, and everyone knew they were clearly directed at his wife. Judging by the muttering of assent from around the room, the other Doms were in complete agreement.

Micah Drake looked toward Kirk, "You and Brian are obviously interested in Regi, but this is likely to bring trouble to your door. Are you prepared for that? Because if you aren't we'll understand." While Kirk understood Micah's concern, he nor Brian were the type to step away from the woman they wanted in their lives just because the ride might get bumpy for a while. Kirk had never had any tolerance for men who walked away from their women when things were challenging, and as physicians specializing in the care of women, they saw it all too often. They could make five times what they were currently bringing in if they'd accept any one of the dozen or so offers they received each month, but they liked their smaller practice.

Knowing each of the women personally made it much easier to treat them effectively. Walking into a small exam room and recognizing their patient, knowing her history and family situation, gave them a huge advantage when providing both preventative and curative care. They'd never walked away from a patient in need, so doing any less for the woman they both wanted was unimaginable.

"I'm not sure exactly how to take that comment, Kyle. But I'm going to assume it is some sort of etiquette bullshit because I can't see that being a serious inquiry. There isn't a chance in hell we'd walk away from Regi, but I think you probably already knew that." When Kyle merely nodded knowingly, Kirk looked at both Kent and Kyle before asking, "Can you send a couple of guys over to clear out her apartment? I'm not sure she'll be thrilled with our highhanded behavior, but I'm not comfortable with her returning there after this."

Kirk saw Jax slide his phone back in his pocket as he looked over from his position near the windows. "Already done. Tank has a key so he'll meet Dex and Ash over there. According to Tank, the place is a hole and she doesn't have much so it'll be a quick in and out. He assured me it would all fit in the back of a pickup." Kirk saw every man in the room flinch and assumed they were wondering the same thing he was...how had the woman they saw every day manage to fly so silently under their radar? Each and every one of them knew one of the most common traits of transient people who were hiding was their minimal personal possessions. They rarely formed attachments to anything they owned because they often had to clear out at a moment's notice, leaving everything behind.

Had her bosses or their security team taken enough of an interest and checked out her living conditions they'd have likely known something was amiss. *Fuck me. Brian and I haven't been any better.* Their knowledge about the every-day life of the woman they wanted to claim was appallingly inadequate, but it was something Kirk vowed to change in short order.

Micah had obviously followed his train of thought when he continued, "Don't even go there, man. None of us knew and I'm assuming the ladies don't know either or they would have clued us in. I just asked Tank why he'd never bothered to let us know the conditions Regi was living in, he told me she'd threatened to cut off their friendship, among other things, if he didn't keep quiet. Tank may not claim to be interested in our lifestyle, but he is a loyal friend and chivalrous to his core. He knew he'd be able to help and look out for her a lot easier if they were close. He also knows where her hidden stash of valuables is so he'll bring that too. Evidently our lovely office manager keeps most of her money in cash."

"No doubt. Much easier to disappear in the middle of the fucking night that way. No waiting for the banks to open and nosey tellers asking why you are withdrawing all that cash from your account." Jax ran his hand through his hair, a clear indicator of his frustration and Kirk understood exactly where he was coming from.

Micah returned his attention to Kirk, "Now the only question is, where they should take her stuff?"

"The small cottage she uses on occasion is open. I'm not sure it would be adequate as a full-time residence, but I want her to know that offer is on the table." It was obvious Kent West didn't expect things to go that way, but Kirk respected the man for making sure everyone knew she was welcome to stay at Prairie Winds despite the danger that might follow her. Considering his wife was due to deliver twins in short order, Kirk understood the true significance of the offer and was sure Regi would as well.

Kirk nodded, "I'll make sure Regi knows, but please ask the men to take everything to our place. The loft has plenty of room for everything and you guys know we spent a lot of time and effort making sure the place is secure." Because they lived in the large loft above their clinic—a clinic with a sizable cache of pharmaceuticals, they'd hired Jax and Micah's security consulting firm to design and install a state of the art security system. Hell, when the thing was activated they knew when tumbleweeds blew down any street within a three-block radius.

Jax snorted a laugh, "That it is, and one of us will be by later tonight to run through a checklist just in case there have been software updates in the last few months. Can't imagine there haven't been, heaven forbid we should leave shit alone. I'll send a scrambler with you until I can get there with a handheld scanner. We'll check over her belongings just in case someone has already been there and planted a bug, but I doubt we'll be that lucky. I can't tell you how much I'd like to backtrack one of those so we could get our hands on whoever is responsible for what happened to her family."

Kirk studied Jax as he leaned a hip against Kyle's desk. Frustration was almost pulsing off the man who was no doubt still reeling from the recent challenges Jen McCall had experienced. She and her new husbands were currently enjoying a working honeymoon on the other side of the world, but Kirk knew Jax had been shaken by how close they had come to losing the young woman they considered part of their family. "I have to tell you, every alarm I have is clanging. There are some big holes in Regi's story. I have a feeling she isn't consciously leaving out anything, but that doesn't mean I'm convinced we aren't missing vital information. I'm anxious to talk to the former agent who helped her and I'll make some additional calls as well." Turning to Kyle he asked, "When you spoke to Hendricks a few months ago you mentioned that you'd gotten the feeling he'd wanted to elaborate, but then he'd backpedaled. Maybe it's time to push him a bit. My gut instinct is that she is telling us everything she thinks is relevant, but that she is discounting something significant."

"I agree, but I'm not sure exactly how to get to it." Micah turned to Peter, "Any suggestions?"

Kirk wasn't entirely sure how comfortable he was having another Dom listening in on Regi's thoughts, but at this point, his concerns for her safety had to outweigh his personal misgivings. He was also intrigued by Peter Weston's gift and more than a little anxious to spend time discussing it with him. Kirk often had fleeting moments where he'd been sure he'd tuned into another person's frequency so he'd had more than a passing interest in the gift. His family had always sworn he'd inherited his Native American ancestor's spiritual gifts, but his entire life had been devoted to science and meshing the two philosophies was a challenge he hadn't really known how to tackle. Having someone to hash it out with was an intriguing prospect.

"I'm not really comfortable delving deeper than what she wants to share with me, even though I'm sure I could. My suggestion is a professional hypnotherapist if you can get her to agree to it. There is always a 'safe-distance' mentality when victims are sharing their story either consciously or unconsciously. When they don't have any personal ties to whoever they are talking to, they have less fear of judgment because a stranger's opinion isn't as important. And even though Regi and I aren't that well acquainted, she knows we'll be working together and might not be comfortable with me knowing so much about her...and quite honestly, I'm not thrilled about damaging our potential friendship or working relationship."

Kirk's respect for the man just jumped exponentially. Peter Weston was obviously a man of integrity, not that he'd doubted it, but seeing it play out right in front of him was a satisfying confirmation. "I don't really know anyone qualified, but I have a feeling that falls right up your guys' alley, so I'll leave you to it. I'll plant a seed as food for thought with Regi, but that's really all I'm willing to do. Brian and I have been trying to build a relationship with her, and I don't want to see that dream die on this battle-field." The other men all nodded in understanding as Kirk made his way to the door. "I'll leave the rest of this to you guys, God knows you're more than prepared for it." They all chuckled at his thinly veiled reference to the fact they'd all been Navy SEALs.

"We've covered Regi's shift tonight so you guys can head out with her right away. She'll need time to settle in tonight. We'll check in with you later and see how things are going. And I suspect Tobi and Gracie will be all over this as well—God save us from pregnant subs armed with cell phones and iPads."

Kent looked at his brother and shook his head, "You're an idiot, you know that? You think we're the only ones with access to the security feeds in this place? Hell, mom, Tobi, and Gracie make our communication systems look archaic." Glancing toward the other men, he chuckled, "I've got three and a half minutes at an even hundred. And a fifty spot on mom."

"Now who's the idiot? I'll take sixty seconds and my

money is on Tobi." This was from Jax who turned to him and grinned, "I happen to know Gracie is taking a nap and that rocket Lilly calls a sports car headed into town just a few minutes ago, which means Tobi is bored and probably standing outside the back door as we speak." Kirk had watched as Jax had moved silently across the room and pulled the door open quickly. He caught Tobi West's well-rounded self when she would have fallen right into the room.

"I swear those babies are going to be in high school before she is caught up on all the punishments she's earned." Kirk was already heading out the other door, but couldn't hold back his laughter at Kyle's words.

If they think they are ever going to be caught up on her punishments they are kidding themselves. I swear the little blonde tigress pushes them just for the fun of it, and damned if everybody doesn't love her for it.

Chapter Four

REGI SAT IN Brian's truck looking out the window as they drove down the Prairie Winds' long drive wondering exactly how she'd managed to lose control of her life in such a remarkably short period of time. Someone needed to explain to her exactly how she'd been outmaneuvered so handedly. Surrendering all of her ability to be self-determining to the wack-a-doodle docs and the fierce foursome Doms at the club because she'd had her head squarely up her ass and they'd insisted she was still "floundering" from her earlier "upset" chapped her ass. *Jesus, Joseph, and Mary, they'd managed to make the whole thing sound fucking Victorian. I almost expected them to pull out the smelling salts and a lace hankie.*

Granted, after telling her story, she'd felt as if someone had just drained all the energy out of her...and when Brian had carried her from the room she hadn't even been able to work up a good mad about his interference, but that didn't mean they should get to call all the shots. She took a deep breath and let it out slowly, trying to get her mind to focus on something...hell, anything for longer than five seconds. If she was honest with herself, she'd admit that she'd actually been so relieved to get out from under their scrutiny she hadn't actually minded being carried, but she certainly didn't plan to share that particular bit of information. No reason to give them the inch she knew they'd turn into a mile.

As they'd walked out of the club, Kirk had casually asked if she thought it was possible she might be unconsciously filtering her memories. She wasn't sure exactly what he'd meant, and now she didn't seem to be able to stop several different possibilities from swirling around in her mind. If he was asking if she might have forgotten something…she didn't see how, because every bit of it had played over in her mind for years. She'd only recently started sleeping through the night, and that was probably going to be a wash for a while again now. Maybe he thought she was intentionally holding back. But that didn't make sense either, because why would she tell them all the most gruesome details and leave out something else that might actually be useful.

The only other possibility she could come up with was that he thought she might have some vital piece of information that she didn't even realize she had…maybe he thought she'd suppressed something or overlooked a detail that hadn't seemed significant to a girl who had just turned sixteen. Could she have missed something potentially significant? Assuming she had anything of value that would explain the family was still tracking her seemed pretty melodramatic if you asked her. Sure she'd known that her sixteenth birthday had been a coming of age point in the family and her parents had warned her many times that her maternal grandmother would likely try to make contact around that time, but that hadn't fit with the extreme violence of the encounter that day on the boat. Those men had been looking for something very specific, and when her mom and dad hadn't handed it over, they'd been killed. Regi felt a shiver race up her spine just as Brian's warm fingers wrapped around her forearm. "Are you cold, baby?"

His touch startled her so badly she actually gasped. "Oh, sweetness, I'm sorry. I knew you were lost in thought, but I didn't realize you were that distracted. Let's see if we can't redirect some of that energy, shall we?" His voice had changed from compassionate to determined. He didn't leave her wondering for long about what he had in mind.

"Open your legs for me, baby. Master Kirk and I will always want to have access to you, so you should get accustomed to riding in this position. There's a good girl, nice and wide." She wanted to protest, but his large hand was caressing the inside of her thigh and all she could think about was how much she wanted to feel his fingers sliding over her clit.

Oh yeah, a killer orgasm would be so much better than a real killer. The absurdity of her thinking would have ordinarily at least made her smile, but nothing above her shoulders seemed to be working right. *But my girl parts seem to be working pretty well, so let's just stick with those for a bit.*

When she heard Brian chuckle she wanted to cringe because she had only meant to speak those words to herself. She let her concern about that slide by as well, because it was so much easier to just...*oh yes, just a bit higher and then a quick pinch and it will be all over but the shouting.* She kept trying to shift so his fingers would hit the sweet spot that would send her over, but he pinched the inside of her leg in warning. She wanted to snarl at him but had the presence of mind to know that wasn't going to get her what she wanted.

Regi only realized then they were already in the small suburb where she knew the good docs' office was located. She'd accompanied both Tobi and Gracie to their appointments and she'd been impressed with the way Brian and Kirk had transformed the older downtown structure.

They'd maintained the integrity of the building's original structure into the design of the clinic and the historical significance of the architectural highlights made it truly spectacular. Tobi had gone on and on about the remarkable job they'd done on their second floor living quarters, but Regi had been grateful both Brian and Kirk had been too busy to give them a tour. Regi wasn't a dimwit. She'd know exactly what Tobi had been up to—the little matchmaker. Once your friends got married, Regi had decided they should be immediately axed from your "pal around with" list because they spent all their time either telling you all the intimate details of their sex lives or trying to hook you up with their new husbands' friends…either way they were a pain in the ass. Chuckling to herself, Regi couldn't help but note the irony of thinking that Tobi West had only become a nuisance *after* she'd gotten married, because that was pure fiction.

Tobi West was a force of nature and Regi had liked her on sight. The petite blonde with the bombshell body and run-to-the-roar attitude had an astonishing ability to work herself into the hearts of everyone she met. There were times Regi had longed for what Tobi had even though she knew it wasn't possible. Kyle and Kent West had fallen fast and hard when Kyle had nearly run over Tobi. Why the woman had thought standing in the middle of the highway during a God awful storm had been a good idea was anyone's guess. But Regi had to give her bosses credit, once they'd gotten their hands on Tobi, they'd held on for all they were worth and never looked back.

Regi pressed her forehead against the truck's window and closed her eyes as a sigh left her lips. Brian's fingers were still tracing teasing patterns on her flesh and she'd given up trying to maneuver him to her sex. "Are you alright, baby?" Brian's tender voice brought her back to the moment. In many ways, Brian Bennett reminded Regi of Kent West. He was, without question, a sexual Dominant, but his approach was often more subtle than Kirk's. That wasn't to say she hadn't been on the receiving end of his no-nonsense methods when she'd pushed back too hard. Both Brian and Kirk had been relentless in their pursuit of her and now they were planning to move her into their home. She'd nearly launched herself into orbit when they'd told her the Prairie Winds team was already moving her belongings out of her dingy little apartment. It wasn't like it was a huge loss, but really…there were times Doms' behavior could just be outrageously overbearing.

Oddly enough, it had been the more rigid Kirk, rather than Brian, who had convinced her that staying alone in an apartment where there wasn't so much as a deadbolt lock was not in her best interest. Hell's bells and sea shells, the truth of the matter was she probably wasn't safe anywhere. And the worst of it was she'd bring that danger to the door of anyone sheltering her as well. She hadn't remembered to answer Brian's question until he gently pinched the tender skin on the inside of her thigh, pulling her back out of her thoughts once again. "I really don't know to be perfectly honest with you. There are so many things bouncing around in my head right now. Remember that crazy sphere Will Smith turns loose in the first *Men in Black* movies? The one that zings wildly through the secret underground headquarters?" When he grinned and nodded, she continued, "Well, that is what is going on inside my head…only there are a bunch of those balls and each one is a different problem I'm trying to track and solve. But they are flying so fast I can't get my hands on one long enough to figure it out." She hadn't even realized they'd stopped until she looked up to see he was gazing at her intently, as if he could pull her back from the emotional edge she was dancing on by the sheer force of his will. *Oh if that were only true.*

REGI HAD BEEN genuinely surprised to see the enormous garage where Kirk and Brian both parked, and even more shocked to see there was a large empty space as well. Kirk had been waiting for them but hadn't opened the truck's passenger door until the large garage door was closed blocking them from view. As he helped her down, he'd pulled her against his chest and tightened his arms around her. Being hugged so securely sent a shudder through her she knew he wouldn't have missed. "Welcome home, *anoshi.*"

Brian was standing by the front of his truck and nodded toward the empty bay next to them. "That space will be for your car, baby. We'll get you a key fob for the door, it will also unlock the elevator." She must have looked surprised because he chuckled, "We are usually bone tired at the end of the day and walking up a steep flight of stairs isn't fun or safe."

Kirk released her and pulled her against his side as he started walking, "Come on. Let's get you settled and fed. And then we'll see what we can do about all that stress I feel coursing through your delectable body." And just like that the air between the three of them sizzled with a charge of pure sexual energy that made the fine hairs on her arm stand up. In ten seconds Kirk had taken her from a warm, safe feeling in his embrace to a pulsing desire that jump started her libido and was already beginning to draw the majority of her focus. *Oh yes, Sir. A couple of scream-the-rafters-down orgasms is just what the doctor ordered...entendre intended!*

REGI FOUND HERSELF enthralled with the elevator. The hinged flat iron bars that unfolded as the gate closed reminded her of the beautiful hotels her parents had taken her as a kid. The only distractions from the old world charm and ambiance were the tiny security cameras in two corners of the overly large enclosure. Kirk pointed out they had needed something akin to a freight elevator to get furniture, appliances, and equipment upstairs so they'd decided to restore the existing service elevator so it was atheistically pleasing so they could keep it as their permanent lift. Listening to the way he spoke...his command of language made her realize how little she really knew about either he or Brian. What was in his background that made him so articulate? She hadn't realized how much she missed hearing a man make those types of comments. Her father had always spoken in much the same way, his appreciation for the beauty he felt surrounded him was apparent in the way he talked about even the simplest things. When she looked up at Kirk, he laughed out loud. "Oh, sunshine, your expressions speak so clearly. And in answer to your unanswered question, my mother is an artisan who taught me to appreciate the finer things in life. She was determined that her offspring would be exposed to a far richer culture than ranch life alone could offer, so we visited museums of all kinds. School breaks were often spent traveling to various exhibits featuring crafts-men...some incredible and some not so much."

When they stepped into the foyer of the loft, Regi gasped at the elegant white marble flooring. The large slabs of marble had rippling veins of onyx meandering through the pristine white marble. The lines reminded her of a winding river looking for the path of least resistance as it makes its way to the sea. The randomness of the pattern was so interesting that Regi didn't even realize she'd stopped until Kirk swatted her. "While we are thrilled you seem fascinated with the floor, you were so lost in thought that you had no earthly idea what was going on around you, and that means your safety was compromised. You'll rack up punishments faster by putting yourself at risk than any other way I can think of, sweetness."

Regi appreciated the fact they were concerned with her safety, but she had been taking care of herself for a very long time. Sure…those pictures were probably a game-changer, but she still didn't appreciate being chastised like a spacy teenager. She set her jaw, but managed to keep her frustration from becoming audible. Pissing off a pair of Doms who were already spoiling for a fight because they were worried about her probably wasn't in her ass's best interest.

Kirk slid the same key fob over a small scanner to activate the door's keypad system and then had tapped in a long series of numbers before she heard the door's lock disengage. Kirk and Brian both dropped their keys in a small glass bowl sitting on a lovely antique oak umbrella stand, which was just inside the enormous carved wooden door. Regi knew they had moved their medical practice from downtown Austin after being robbed several times, so she'd expected them to have a good security system…but this was far above anything she'd envisioned.

They had obviously invested a lot of time and money

renovating and remodeling the building they'd purchased. The living space's wooden floors were a deep, rich blending of a variety of darker shades and it was shined to perfection. Regi had a vision of herself sliding across the floor in her stocking feet lip-synching like Tom Cruise. She tried to push back the thought of all the disastrous ways her uncoordinated self could wipe out. Instead of looking cool, she'd look more like a human bowling ball knocking over everything in her path. *Probably need to scratch the Risky Business moves and just worry about keeping your feet under you.*

The walls of the open-space design had been left as resurfaced brick and the effect was a nod to the second and third floor's original use as storage for the dry goods store on the first level. But the thing that caught her eye was a series of prints displayed on one wall. The pictures and frames were an eclectic mix of old and new, but the theme was unmistakable. How had they known? She'd just shared her story a few hours ago so there hadn't been any time for them to tailor this display to her, but it seemed just too coincidental to be true.

Regi had been so engrossed in studying the pictures, she hadn't realized for several minutes that Brian was standing along her right side. He wasn't touching her, but he was close enough the warmth radiating from him warmed her bare arm. The earthy scent of his aftershave tinted with sage wrapped itself around her and she felt herself calming despite her surprise. He didn't take his eyes off the pictures, but she knew he was speaking to her. "I've always loved ships, particularly those with sails. My mother was born and raised in New England. Her family is still there for the most part."

Regi was surprised to realize how much she wanted to get to know both men. And even though she knew they still held on to the ludicrous idea that the three of them could build a life together. *Who on earth would want to hook up with me? Nobody with even the finest thread of common sense wants to deal with "the family"*. Charlie had warned her about the dangers associated with emotional entanglements until the price was lifted from her head. And she had religiously avoided them prior to taking the job at the Prairie Winds Club. She'd thought working in a secluded place where confidentiality was so highly valued was a job custom-made for her, but she'd made friends…really close friends, even when she had tried to keep her distance. Those crazy people had wormed themselves right into her heart despite all her lofty claims about staying detached. *Fuck a tuxedoed turtle, I'm so screwed.*

Chapter Five

K IRK WAS CERTAIN he'd never met a submissive whose
face displayed her emotions in more vivid detail than
Regina Turner's. He'd stood to the side, leaning against
one of their expansive living room's brick outer walls with
his arms crossed over his chest as he studied her intently.
Watching her speak with Brian about the collection of
pictures his friend had been putting together for as long as
Kirk could remember was like getting a sneak peek into her
soul. After hearing her story earlier today, it wasn't
surprising she'd been immediately drawn to the prints. Kirk
had been sailing on several occasions, and while he enjoyed
it, he didn't share Brian's deep love of the sea. Kirk had
always felt his love of the southwest was deeply seeded in
his DNA. His Native American heritage had been diluted
over the generations, but he still felt a close connection
with Mother Earth.

It was still very early evening and ordinarily Regi's
workday would be far from over, but the lines of exhaustion were clearly etched in her sweet face. Kirk had heard
some of the other club members refer to Regi as "elfin" but
he preferred the term petite. His Apache grandmother had
made sure all of her grandchildren knew the stories of their
ancestors and that included knowing all the traits of the
mystical creatures, so he'd shied away from the term he'd
associated with more negative qualities. His *shiichoo* had

told her grandchildren stories from her own Apache culture and her beloved's Navajo people as well. Kirk had understood from an early age that while the languages and art might be different, both cultures shared a deep love for their traditions, families, and the Great Spirit.

Each time they'd played with Regi, he and Brian had made concerted efforts to stay mindful of how much smaller she was than either of them. At six foot two, Kirk was only two inches shorter than Brian, but they were both well over a foot taller than Regi's five foot nothing. Even though she was short, it had always taken effort to remember how small she was because her personality had always seemed so large.

Regi had fooled them for quite a while with her outsized personality and *in your face* attitude. It had only been during her most unguarded moments of passion while they played that they'd begun to see fissures in the façade. Then Micah had warned them others were concerned the foundation was beginning to crumble out from under her, and his words had been a validation of their concerns.

There was still something niggling at the back of his mind about her story—he knew there was some detail he was missing. He hated the feeling that an answer he was seeking was just out of his reach. If there had been any chance they could get away, he'd take Regi to see his *shiichoo*. His Apache grandmother was well known in their community for her healing gifts, what wasn't well known was the true depth of her spiritual gifts. But he and Brian both had several patients with babies due at any time, including Tobi and Grace. And as protective as their Dom friends were, there would be hell to pay if any other doctor delivered those babies.

Shiichoo teased him that he'd became a doctor as a way

to attribute his own healing gifts to science. Kirk had in turn teased the older woman about her numerous warnings about the evils of relying on "only those things you can see". Oddly enough, her words had seemed to come to mind often since he'd met Regi and he wondered if perhaps that in itself was a message.

Unfortunately, the real reason he and his best friend had decided to become doctors was far less altruistic. When they'd been undergrads, he and Brian dreamt of making big money and enjoying all the perks that youth associates had with that lifestyle. They'd seen the movie *Doc Hollywood* but they'd managed to miss the real message. The movie had steered them toward becoming plastic surgeons because they'd seen their escape from the hard work of ranching and the lifelong commitment it required for success. They weren't fools—they knew the effect they had on women, and they'd plotted and planned to exploit it ruthlessly.

The two of them had spent many nights detailing how they would build a successful medical practice catering to the rapidly growing number of middle age women whose vanity was fed by their dedication to careers, paying enough to justify their desire to look and feel attractive. And if fooling around a bit with a hot doc who was happy to feed fantasy loosened the purse strings…all the better. It was the perfect plan—big money and lots of sex. But one late night phone call had changed everything.

The death of Brian's younger sister, Beth, had been a senseless tragedy. If she had gotten appropriate pre-natal care, both Beth and her unborn son would not have been laid to rest on that cold February afternoon. Standing beside her family at the gravesite, Kirk would have sworn his heart was being torn from his chest because he'd always felt she was his little sister too. The overwhelming sense of loss and grief had felt like a living, breathing entity. Kirk's own family had also been in attendance that day since the two families had been friends going back several generations, and looking over at his mom as she held her sobbing friend in her arms had been a defining moment...how easily it could have been his own sister who had failed to get care.

The Bennett's hadn't approved of Beth's husband and in their misguided efforts to bring the young woman to heel, they'd stopped providing financial support for the two college students. And because her husband cared more about feeding his drug habit than he did caring for the two people he was supposed to love above all others, Beth hadn't had the money to seek the specialized prenatal care required for diabetic patients. It still scalded Kirk's ass that the jerk hadn't been held accountable, even though he believed in the "Rule of Three," he wasn't sure he wanted to wait long enough for the man's negative actions to return to him three-fold.

Refocusing his attention on the beautiful woman standing in his living room, Kirk heard Brian admonish Regi when she complimented them on how beautiful *their* home was. "This is your home now too, sweetness. If you forget that again there will be consequences. Do you understand?" Kirk held back his smile because the look on her face told him she was surprised by this side of the Master she'd thought was the more lenient of the two of them. It was actually a common misconception, people were fooled by Brian's blonde surfer-dude appearance, taking it for a personality trait when in fact Brian was far stricter about protocol then he was. Kirk considered it a testament to how well they worked together that Regi hadn't picked up the difference during their previous scenes.

"Yes, but I wasn't trying to be—" Brian's hand connected with her deliciously rounded ass with a resounding thwack that silenced her immediately. Kirk saw her gaze flick to him, but he kept his expression completely neutral. When she looked back at Brian, he was just peering down at her with a brow raised—waiting. "Well, drown me…" *Thwack, thwack.*

This time Kirk wasn't able to hold back his chuckle as he pushed off from the wall and started toward them, "Regi, I think you know how to properly answer a Master. And I think it is in your lovely backside's best interest if you do it right this next time." He and Brian had always worked under the premise of "begin as you intend to go" and that was obviously where Brian was headed now.

Kirk grinned when he saw her look down but he had the distinct impression she was pulling together her patience more than she was slipping into a submissive mind-set. She didn't say anything for a few seconds— precious time Kirk knew were going to cost her several stinging swats and sure enough, Brian gave her three in rapid succession. Her gasp told him there had been more power behind the latest strokes and they had their desired effect because her quick, "Yes, Sir, I understand" was probably out before she even realized she'd spoken.

Stepping up in front of Regi, he looked down into eyes that were usually filled with fire and mischief, but today she just looked lost and scared. And as much as he wanted to pull her into his arms and tell her everything would be fine, that wasn't what she needed right now. In this moment she needed their strength because she obviously didn't think she had any left. Her uncertainty showed in her expression and he knew if they could empower her, show her that she could fight back against the fear, they'd have a chance of making her theirs forever. As he saw it, they had two foes in this battle. The first was the group she'd referred to as "the family", and the second was the more formidable in his opinion, and that was the ice princess standing in front of him. She'd isolated herself for so long they were going to have to proceed carefully, but they also had to break through those barriers one at a time. He'd seen Doms break through a submissive's barriers one week, only to have to start from the beginning the next time they played, so personally he thought they'd be better off burning Regi's clear to the ground. It would be much more difficult to reassemble ashes than broken blocks.

BRIAN WATCHED AS the fragile young girl still buried inside Regi battled the strong woman she'd become, each wanting to take the reins, but neither gaining the upper hand. What neither of those sides knew was that he and Kirk had already picked up the reins and they were damn well planning to keep them in hand. There wasn't any doubt they were selfish bastards where Regi was concerned. She wasn't ready to accept the fact she belonged to them, so they had to proceed carefully, but at the same time he also sensed an underlying urgency that was impossible to ignore.

He could hardly wait to show her the top floor. He and Kirk both had bedroom suites that could be easily converted to other uses on the main floor of their loft home. But they'd created a master suite on the third floor that was as unique as it was spectacular. They'd basically created an outdoor garden oasis and then erected glass walls around it. Portions of the floor was made up of split planks and river rock covered by resin so even though the surface was smooth to protect a woman's bare feet, it gave the illusion of walking outside. The hot tub in the corner looked like a steaming mineral spring surrounded by large river rocks fronted by a stone fireplace that was open on the three sides. One side of the fireplace was visible from the hot tub, another side faced a small sitting area with leather-upholstered furniture specifically designed for dual uses, and the third side opened toward the enormous pedestal bed.

Brian had designed the bed and then worked with the same craftsmen that had created so many of the Prairie Winds Club's pieces. Clint Bollinger and the men at E.G.A. Fabrication in Sealy had taken Brian's ideas and created an amazing work of metal artistry with hidden treasures any Master would be thrilled with. Not only was the intricate design flush with erotic scenes hidden in what looked like a forest scene, there were various anchors for restraints and sliding hoists built into what appeared to be nothing more than an elaborately draped canopy. The bed itself was well grounded because Brian had a particular fondness for violet wands and regularly used them as both rewards and *punishment* during scenes. Brian didn't use the implements for any real punishment because he'd never wanted a sub in his care to fear the device that could stimulate them in such sensual ways.

Two walls of the room were actually a series of large sliding glass panels that could be opened remotely giving the room an outdoor quality. There weren't a lot of days and nights when the weather in the Texas hill country was perfect, but they planned to take advantage of each and every one. Their rooftop shared some similarities with the one Kyle West had designed, because Kyle had guided them in their project. The most significant difference was they hadn't intended their beautiful oasis to be used for entertaining anyone but the three of them, so the only access to the garden area was through the master suite. Despite the fact both he and Kirk considered their club friends their second family, that didn't mean they wanted them traipsing through the room they planned to share with their wife.

Redirecting his thoughts to the woman he hoped would fill that role, Brian heard her small gasp as Kirk stepped up and calmly commanded, "Give me your panties, *anoshi*." Her eyes went wide, her surprise obvious, but the sudden hitch in her breathing gave away the fact she was aroused. The short halter dress she'd worn to work would still cover her delicious ass, but Brian knew Kirk's command was about the psychological effect of being bare under the dress rather than any actual physical exposure. Her hesitation was going to be something they'd be addressing in the near future, but until she was settled a few swats would have to suffice. Since Kirk was standing directly in front of Regi, Brian was happy to do the honors.

"Sweetness, you are not new to the lifestyle so there is no reason for you to delay in following Master Kirk's order. Now, we told you we were going to eat before we played…and personally, I'd love to see you sitting at the table naked. But I'm not sure you're ready for that much exposure just yet, so give Master Kirk your panties before he decides to ask for your dress as well." He watched as she reached under the full skirt and slowly drew the miniscule scrap of elastic and lace, that his fingertips had brushed against in the truck, down her well-toned legs. She'd dropped her gaze but Brian could see her jaw flexing as she battled to not voice her frustration with their heavy-handed behavior.

It was obvious her efforts hadn't escaped Kirk's notice because Brian could see his friend was fighting back a smile. "In the future, delays will be punished as will your obvious reluctance to obey." When she dangled the light blue thong from her fingertip, Kirk took them from her and brought the undergarment to his nose. Inhaling deeply, he smiled, "I love the way you smell, *anoshi*. Your essence calls to me in a way I can't find words to describe."

Kirk stuffed them into his pocket as Regi asked, "What does that mean? You have called me *anoshi* a couple of times during scenes and I've never known what it meant." When Kirk merely looked at her with his brow cocked, she realized her mistake and amended her question, adding a hasty "Sir" before looking between the two of them.

"It is what my father calls my mother, it means 'my love' in the Navajo language. My father's ancestors were from different nations so I learned bits and pieces of both languages from my grandmother." When she opened her mouth to protest such an intimate endearment, Brian wanted to laugh at how easy she was to read. Kirk quickly pressed a finger against her lips, "Think carefully before you speak, little sub. Is what you want to say worth the price you will pay for it?" Brian smiled when acceptance moved over her face and then slid over her like a slow moving wave. He loved the way her entire body seemed to relax when she started letting go and began slipping into the submissive state of mind they were after. They hoped to begin showing her that completely embracing her submission—where she wouldn't have any decisions to make and none of the battles she'd been fighting would be hers to win alone—would set her free in ways she had yet to fully experience.

Regi finally took a deep breath and Brian was pleased to hear her barely whispered, "No, Sir." When she looked over at him, Brian felt his breath catch at the lost look that filled her eyes. Her bright green eyes were usually filled with sass and fire, but today they were filled with worry and a soul-deep fatigue that belied the fact she was a very young woman. At twenty-six she should be thinking about her future in terms of decades rather than days.

What Regi had been shouldering was enough to send the strongest people he knew into a tailspin, but for a submissive it meant a daily battle against the very core of what he or she was because it was the antithesis of what they lived for. A true submissive lived to serve, they blossomed when they were cared for and cherished. Submissives were often seen as "pleasers" and inaccurately viewed as weak when in fact it takes enormous courage to surrender to another.

In Brian's view, he and Kirk would face two major problems with Regi. The first was the fact the walls she'd erected to protect herself from the outside world had been in place for a very long time, their strength and depth wouldn't be easy to breach. The second was the fact she had been redirecting her soul's yearning to serve for so long, Brian suspected it would feel alien for her to step out from behind the mask she'd been wearing for years.

Chapter Six

REGI SAT ON one of the high bar stools at the kitchen bar and watched as the two doctors prepared dinner. They clearly knew their way around a kitchen and worked together in what looked like a well-choreographed and often practiced routine. Kirk had made her pull up her skirt so her bare ass was against the wood, and Brian had pulled her knees apart showing her how to hook her ankles around the front legs of the stool reminding her of their discussion in his truck. They had both nodded in approval and told her that was the way they always wanted her to sit when eating unless they specifically told her otherwise. Because her dress had a full skirt she wasn't exposed to view, but she was certainly much more "available" to their touch and both men took full advantage of the access. It seemed to her as if one of them was touching her almost continually. It was if they were tag teaming to imprint the feel of their hands on her, and it was both comforting and frightening.

She'd always been a very tactile person and had gotten even more so while working at the club. Tank was very affectionate and had never recoiled from her spontaneous hugs. Tobi West hadn't received any physical affection after her mother had died, but she was making up for lost time in a huge way. Regi laughed to herself as the thought about all the changes she'd seen in Tobi since they'd first met. *The little blonde tornado practically glows from the inside out and holy crap on a cactus, she is a flipping hugging machine.* Brian's fingers sliding between her thighs brought Regi back to the moment.

"I don't know where you went, baby, but it looked like you were enjoying the trip. Care to share?" Regi wasn't fooled by Brian's benign tone, she knew an order when she heard one no matter how diplomatically it was phrased.

"Actually, I was thinking about how much I have enjoyed being touched by you. It has been distracting and I needed that...but I suppose you already knew that, didn't you? Anyway, that led me to think about Tobi and how she didn't have anyone to hug her when she was a kid and she had all those awful experiences with her dad and now she hugs everybody all the time like she is trying to make up for lost time and..." She had actually been starting to get dizzy she was so out of breath, and didn't know how much more she would have managed to spit out if Brian hadn't pressed his lips against hers.

Regi felt as if she'd been shoved into a wooden barrel and pushed over Niagara Falls. The clattering noises that were bouncing around inside her head were an annoying blend of the clackity-clack old wooden roller coasters made and rappity-rap of clog dancers...a lot of clog dancers. *Holy hell all the wooden shoes in Holland wouldn't make all this noise.*

They had done scenes together a few times at the club and then there had been one incredible night after the McCall's wedding, but all things considered, neither of the men had kissed her often. But *this* was a knock your socks off, curl your toes in your shoes kiss. She'd heard the other subs at the club talking about Masters who could make time stop with their kisses and since she'd never experienced it firsthand she had blown it off as romantic fantasy.

She shouldn't have discounted their words because Brian Bennett's kiss was soul stealing in its intensity. It had been a full-court press from the instant their lips touched, something she would have expected from Kirk rather than Brian.

His lips were soft but firm and sealed against hers hard and fast. His tongue slid along the seam of her lips and she opened to him without hesitation. He didn't waste the invitation, exploring every inch of her mouth. Brian tasted like the sweet wine they'd been sipping with a hint of wild promises she suspected would always be the underlying tone of his kisses. Her nipples responded and the sensitive tips were pushing against the soft fabric of her dress and her body instinctively arched so her breasts pressed against his chest. She wanted more…and at this point it wouldn't take much for her to fall all the way into a mindless release that she knew would let her escape the insanity that she was drowning in…at least for a few precious minutes.

Many nights she had laid on the thin mattress she'd put on the floor of her apartment and tried to lull herself to sleep despite the deafening noise from the family living above her. She usually tried to lose herself in her carefully constructed fantasies of Brian and Kirk. She'd been able to almost feel the sweet caress of their lips as they brushed over her body like a feather dancing in a summer breeze. But there wasn't anything remotely featherlike in this kiss. This kiss screamed desire and possession. It was all about staking a claim.

The only thing Regi knew at this moment was that she really didn't know anything at all. She was floating in a sweet flood of desire and Brian's kiss sent a tidal wave of happy endorphins racing through her body. *Oh my, not knowing anything is not so bad after all.* A fleeting moment of amusement raced through her mind at the fact her mother's fascination with Socrates had echoed through her mind during a moment of unrestrained physical response but the observation was quickly buried by unbridled lust. Anytime Regi had asked her mother a question about the cosmos or anything vaguely philosophical, her mom had quoted the ancient Greet philosopher, Socrates… *The only thing I know for certain is that I know nothing at all.* It hadn't been until this moment that Regi had fully understood his words, but as Brian Bennett proceeded to scramble her brain with his kiss, she could certainly relate.

He was thrusting his tongue into her mouth giving her a preview of coming attractions. As soon as she was able to form a coherent thought, Regi realized she'd tightened her fists in the front of his shirt and she'd used the leverage to press herself up against him so close she could feel the buttons of his shirt pressing into her breast. She moaned against his plundering mouth when she tried to get closer but there wasn't any distance to close. When his hands closed over her ass cheeks and squeezed, Regi used his strength to tilt back and press her pelvis against his erection. It wasn't the action of a trained submissive—no, it was the instinctive response of a woman free falling into a deep blue churning whirlpool of lust. Her brain was just beginning to demand oxygen when he pulled back, leaving her gasping. It felt like the room was spinning and her disquiet must have shown because Brian cupped both sides of her head stilling everything inside her that was screaming to hold on because the world was tilting.

"I'm not sure what it's going to take to get you out of your head, baby. But I can promise you we're all going to enjoy the hell out of everything we try while we're searching for it." Brian's soft tone was such a sharp contrast to his balls-to-the-wall kiss that Regi found herself wanting to shake the cobwebs of confusion out of her mind. With those words Brian uncurled her fists from his shirt with gentle fingers and then stepped aside. Kirk filled the space in front of her and she was surprised to see the wanton expression in his eyes, obviously he'd enjoyed watching his best friend kiss her.

Before she'd taken the job at the club, Regi would have considered being with two men at the same time well beyond anything she could handle...both emotionally and physically. It wasn't that she was judgmental, because God only knew that with a family background like hers, she was one of the last people in a position to look down on someone else. But the easy acceptance of other people and the respect she'd seen for a vast array of *kinks* by all the club's members had opened Regi's eyes in many ways. The soft brush of Kirk's fingers over her cheek brought her focus back to him. He registered her attention and smiled. "Don't ever let anyone tell you how to feel, *anoshi*. As Doms we'll make a lot of demands, and among those will be for you to be more aware of what you are feeling. We'll also insist that you are completely honest with us and yourself about what you are experiencing—both inside and outside our scenes. But we'll never condemn or judge you."

How had he known? Is everything I'm thinking suddenly scrolling across my forehead like those bright digital marquees that are everywhere? Geez, if I fuck somebody who can see inside my head, they are going to run screaming off into the night. Nobody wants that shit floating around in their head. Damn...damn...double damn. The stinging swat to her ass caused her to gasp.

"As much as I'd like to be able to crawl inside your head I can't. It's true that I am an empath and I'm better at hearing you than I am with most people. And while I'm sure my sweet grandmother will have a hay-day reminding me of all the reasons our connection is particularly strong, I'm fairly certain I already know the answer." Regi knew he'd paused so his words could settle in, and it had taken her a few seconds to catch up. She'd lived alone for so long she often found herself existing in a mental cocoon and had frequently wondered at the lasting effect that would have if she was ever free to pursue a relationship. But that safe place in her head was often a quagmire, and being yanked back this suddenly frequently required her mind to shift gears faster than she could manage, particularly when she was overly tired or stressed. He had obviously read that need and accommodated her.

"I want to remind you—we will always focus first and foremost on providing you with what you *need* whether that is protection, confidence, a shoulder to cry on, or to simply be held. We'll also provide punishment and discipline when they are warranted. It's likely you won't always agree with our judgment, but you will come to trust it nonetheless. I think you already trust us even though you don't really fully understand why. But the only thing you can count on, *anoshi*, is that our decisions are made with your best interests at heart...always."

Regi's head was spinning again, but this time it was the apparent expectation of a future she couldn't allow herself to even consider. She didn't want to make either of them angry by disagreeing, but she wasn't going to dream of something she couldn't have because walking away would hurt so much more. *It's much easier to not dream of what could be than it is to have my hopes slashed. The Queen of Denial...that's me.*

REGI MIGHT THINK she was getting away with all her wayward thoughts, but Kirk was just keeping a tab as he listened to the bullshit tumbling through her mind. At first he'd been so in awe of the fact he could "hear" her so clearly he'd nearly missed the significance of her jumbled thoughts. He wondered how her thinking had become so skewed, but then he remembered she'd essentially been on her own since she was sixteen. She hadn't had parents to guide and protect her while navigating the years when those role models could make the biggest difference. The occasional contact she'd had with one federal agent wouldn't have been nearly enough to make her truly believe in her value as a person. The hole he could feel in her heart brought his urge to shelter and protect her roaring to the forefront. Those feelings weren't entirely new to him, he felt the same with the other subs at the club, his female family members, friends, and patients. But the intensity of those feelings with Regi were so exponentially magnified they were starting to overrun his good sense. Pulling his thoughts back into line, Kirk stepped back from her. "Since we'll be living together, we need to reconsider the parameters of our D/s relationship. We will be playing here at home and won't be bound by the same rules we've followed at Prairie Winds."

He registered her moment of panic when it flashed through her expression so he quickly forged ahead. "Safe, sane, and consensual will always be our guiding tenant, Regi. With that in mind, we'd like you to continue to use the club's stop light system as your safe word. If you say the word *red* at any time during a scene, everything will come to an immediate stop. We'll take as much time as we need to figure out what went wrong and how to remedy the situation. Yellow means you need a moment to catch your breath or ask a question. We will listen, but we may or may not change what we're doing."

He could tell she was relaxing again as he reviewed the rules that he knew she had explained to new club members hundreds of times. There would be many times they would intentionally keep her off balance because that was what it was going to take to break through her barriers, but he wasn't planning to push her too hard just yet. Tonight needed to be about the three of them settling in to their new arrangement.

"Are you on birth control?" Kirk hadn't expected the blank stare Regi gave him in answer to what he'd thought was a simple question. But her deer in the headlights look let him know he'd surprised her, and her red flush of embarrassment surprised him. *Why would a woman in today's society, particularly one who works in a kink club, be embarrassed when asked about birth control? Unless...oh Jesus, Joseph, and Mary. Brian is going to go fucking postal...*

"Well, no, I'm not. I get my blood tests like all the other club members, but I haven't gotten birth control yet. I haven't really needed it...and well, I don't really have a regular doctor or anything..." Kirk could see she was trying to dance around the truth. She was taking great care to avoid lying, and from the look on Brian's face he'd figured out the truth of it as well.

Brian stepped forward so quickly Regi instinctively stepped back. Kirk watched his best friend take a calming breath before speaking, "Regi, when was the last time you had a complete physical?" Kirk knew what a hot point this was for his friend and suspected Regi was quickly figuring that out as well because she had suddenly become very interested in the floor. *Like either of us will ever let you get away with that lame ass attempt to hide.* Brian used the tips of his fingers to raise her chin until she was forced to look directly at him. "Don't even consider lying to us, baby. And remember, editing your answer will net you a punishment just as quickly as lying will. Now, when was your last physical, aside from the pre-employment screening, which I'm sure was little more than a blood test and blood pressure check."

Kirk shifted so he was close enough to lay his palm over the lower portion of her back, right atop the spot where the curve of her gorgeous ass began. He'd heard several subs mention how that simple gesture could calm and reassure them because it reminded them their Master was in control and the only thing expected of them was compliance. He had actually spoken with Noelle Chambers about it one evening when she and her husband, Neal, had joined them for dinner. Noelle was a prosecutor in Austin and her direct communication style often challenged her Dom's patience. Dr. Neal Chambers was the pediatrician he and Brian most often referred their patients to because he was one of the best in the area. Kirk admired Neal and Noelle's ability to integrate the lifestyle into their lives when they were both dedicated to stressful careers that more often than not kept them far busier than they wanted to be.

Noelle had explained how different types of touch affected a sub. She'd described the feeling as being "anchored" by her Master's palm against the small of her back whether he was gently guiding her through a crowd or simply making the contact as they stood talking to friends. Both he and Brian had been transfixed by her words because they'd neither one ever considered the power of that particular touch. She'd laughed at them telling them there was a difference in knowing about a woman's body as a doctor and knowing about one as a Dom. The stern look she'd gotten from Neal had amused him because Kirk had been fairly sure the little brat had been angling for a paddling. Her Master was well versed in all the creative ways she found to top from the bottom and rarely let it slide for long.

Neal had once told him that he used the behavior as a barometer in their relationship, it was his sweet sub's way of letting him know she needed his help. Noelle's job required her to be strong and *on* all the time, and even though she loved her career, it also caused internal conflict with the submissive side of her personality. Her bratty behavior told Neal when she needed his strong hand in order to bring everything inside her back into alignment, and that only happened for her during intense scenes.

As he watched Regi closely, he was astounded to see how true Noelle's words had been. The effects of that simple touch had been immediate and unmistakable. The empath in him could actually feel her let go and the outward effect was almost as dramatic. Regi's muscles went from "fight or flight" mode to calm in the span of several heartbeats. Kirk made a mental note to ask Neal's permission to send his helpful wife a thank you gift for her insight.

What Kirk heard next could not have surprised him more. Regi looked up at Brian and with a completely straight face asked, "You're not going to go all Dr. Wack-a-Doodle on me, are you? Because if you are I think I'll just 'plead the fifth' and call it a day." The look on Brian's face was priceless and even though her insolence was going to cost her dearly, Kirk wanted to hug her for taking what had been a really pivotal moment and lightening it in a way only Regi could pull off.

"What. The. Fuck. Does. That. Mean?" Brian's words were spoken through clenched teeth and it was obvious to Kirk he was struggling to maintain his Dom persona and not burst out laughing at her cheeky use of the nickname they'd already heard she'd given them.

To her credit, Regi did suddenly look contrite. Kirk assumed she probably realized the full potential of her comments since they'd already given her clear indication their scene had started. And even though neither he nor Brian were interested in living the D/s lifestyle twenty-four seven, they would always expect a sub in their care to show them a certain level of respect, and they would show her the same. But Regi's response would be considered coloring outside the lines by even the most lenient Dom and she damned well knew it. "Oh shit."

Kirk gave her two swats hard enough to send her up onto her toes. "Oh shit, indeed. We'll deal with your punishment for that in a bit, but first—answer your Master's question—and check the attitude."

Regi gulped and tried to turn her face away out of Brian's grip, but he held her firmly in hand. "I haven't…well, I don't really remember when I last had a real doctor's appointment. I mean, I don't have insurance right now and doctors charge a lot, you know?" When she realized what she'd said and to whom, she reminded him of a balloon that had suddenly started to leak air. "Drown me. I didn't mean that to sound disrespectful, but I just haven't had the extra money and I'm always working when they have the local health fairs. And you are the only doctors I really know and well…I was afraid if you knew you would insist on doing it for free and I didn't want to be a charity case or anything. Tobi and Gracie have been bitching at me for months about this same thing and to be honest, I'm kind of surprised they hadn't already ratted me out."

Even though she'd been rattling on, Kirk was grateful because it had given Brian a chance to pull himself back together. Good Lord, the past few minutes with Regi had been like riding a pendulum that was swinging between wanting to paddle her until she wouldn't sit comfortably for a week and amusement at her cheekiness. Neither of them would ever punish a submissive while they were angry so Kirk appreciated the short reprieve, because if there was ever a sub in need of a good paddling, it was the one in front of him. Of course they'd be using the snarky comment and the fact she wasn't taking proper care of herself as an excuse, but the bottom line was she was struggling against her own scattered thoughts and giving her something else to focus on would probably bring her more relief than pain...eventually. He fought back his smile as Brian turned and abruptly walked from the room. Kirk knew where his friend was headed and exactly what he'd be bringing back with him, but Regi's entire body was shouting her uncertainty.

Kirk watched her closely as she started wringing her hands and pacing. Her tiny bare feet padding softly on the wood floor of the kitchen. "Well shit. Way to piss off your host, Regina. Didn't your mother teach you any manners at all? And annoying a Dom is just stupid. They have all sorts of ways to punish subs you know...dumb...very, very dumb. And all because you wouldn't spend the money to go to a fanny doc and let him look into your hoohah. Didn't want just anybody looking at your girly parts so you didn't go at all and now look where that's gotten you."

It was fascinating to watch, even though he was beginning to feel like a peeping Tom. Kirk wondered briefly if this was something she did regularly or if he and Brian were bringing out the crazy in her. His snort of laughter stopped her dead in her tracks. Even though he'd been laughing at himself, she was clearly mortified. When her eyes filled with tears Kirk stepped around the counter and pulled her into his arms. *"Mi amõre,* I wasn't laughing at you. I was actually worried that we were the ones causing your meltdown." He felt her freeze in his arms and when he pulled her back so he could look into her eyes, he was surprised to see them filled with remorse.

"No, you have both been really kind. I haven't been very nice to you and I'm not even sure why you still want me around. I'm a pain in the ass and God only knows what trouble is going to darken your door with me here. And I don't want you to think I'm not grateful that you've given me a place to live, because I really am. I just couldn't stay at Prairie Winds when there will be children there soon. I'd never forgive myself if anything ever happened to anyone because of me." Kirk understood what she was saying, but her mistake had been trying to make all the choices on her own. She had almost unimaginable resources as her fingertips, but hadn't had the courage to ask for help. It spoke clearly of her past and the struggles she'd been through—but it needed to end and he knew that was a large part of what Brian was planning to do now. The punishment Kirk had in mind wouldn't be particularly easy for her. But Regi definitely needed a lesson in the value of allowing others to help her.

"Has anyone ever told you that denying others the opportunity to help you is very selfish?" Kirk saw all the emotions play out in her expression as clearly as if she'd narrated them. At first she'd been shocked at being called selfish. He knew that was an abomination to a true submissive because it was their nature to give far more than they ever took. Then she'd been puzzled about how he'd managed to see her that way. Finally her mind had rebelled against that assessment…and *that* was exactly where he'd wanted her to be. It was better to have her angry than feeling defeated. She would have a much better chance of staving off the emotional freefall she'd been fighting from a position of strength than one of weakness. Sometimes empowering another person didn't look like that on the surface. But he'd much rather see the fire in her eyes than the look of defeat he'd seen a few minutes ago.

"I know you don't understand it all now, but you will. But first, we have a punishment to get through." When his phone buzzed, he glanced at the screen. Reading the short text telling him the men who had cleaned out Regi's apartment would be arriving in just a few minutes, he wanted to smile at their timing. *Perfect*.

Chapter Seven

R EGI'S EYES WENT wide when Brian walked back into the room carrying a small duffle. He knew she wouldn't know specifically what he'd chosen, but she'd certainly worked at the club long enough to know a Dom's toy bag could hold a large array of possibilities. Her beautiful green eyes glazed just a bit when he set the bag on the counter beside her. He'd been able to hear most of the conversation she'd had with Kirk, and knew she'd already been talked off the ledge of panic once so he didn't want to drag this out. He'd answered the text message he and Kirk had both gotten announcing Dex Raines and Ash Moore's imminent arrival, and set things up for their scene. The timing was perfect and the only hurdle had been the fact Tank had been with them.

Brian stepped back, crossed his arms over his chest, and simply watched her for long seconds. He could see she was trying to keep her gaze lowered, but those curious eyes had lost their earlier glaze and now they kept darting to the bag before returning to the floor. Her breathing had sped up and her pulse was racing at the base of her throat as the flush of arousal began to spread over her ivory skin. "Look at me, Regi." When her gaze met his he continued, "Take down your hair. Hand me the pins and don't finger comb it or try to otherwise control it." He wasn't about to tell her how much he loved the curls and waves she tried so desperately to tame. Her hands trembled as she raised them and began pulling out the pins that held the auburn silk neatly off her neck and face. Watching the rope of hair unroll and spill over her shoulder was one of the hottest things he'd ever seen. She placed the pins in his upturned palm and he wondered how she'd managed to secure all those lovely waves with just a few pieces of bent metal.

The temptation to abandon the plan he'd put in place was pushing Brian into unfamiliar territory. He and Kirk were both known as strict, but fair, Doms. There were no surprises when they played with a submissive. They always negotiated scenes carefully and never strayed from what they had all agreed upon. Nice and safe. Predictable. Before Regi, it had worked. But now? Looking back it was clear that everything they'd done was just a prelude to this woman. When he thought back on the women they'd paddled, flogged, and fucked, he was amazed their faces had dimmed from his memory. His life as a sexual Dominant was definitely going to be defined as pre- and post-Regi eras.

"Before we begin, I want you to know the men delivering your things will be here in just a few minutes. Tank is with them but he won't be entering our living space." He'd deliberately used the word *our* so she would start thinking of this as her home, not just a temporary shelter until the storm passed. "We understand the importance of the boundary between you and Tank. He is not a Dom and has no particular interest in the lifestyle. That alone is enough reason for us to exclude him from what we have planned, but the bottom line is—the two of you are friends and co-workers. That relationship is important to you and we won't do anything to compromise it."

Her narrow shoulders relaxed and he saw her eyes fill

with tears. Brian saw Kirk stiffen beside him and then relax when she whispered, "Thank you, Sir."

Brian nodded once in acknowledgment and then let his eyes look down over her body in a slow perusal. Regi was so responsive that he knew she would feel his eyes move over her almost as if he'd actually touched her. They'd made her leave her shoes by the door and he wanted to smile at the pale pink polish she'd chosen for the tips of her toes. Most of the subs at the club used bold colors. He'd often thought their choices were garish. He usually dismissed it as an attempt to express themselves in an environment that often required them to be restrained both physically and emotionally until their Dom gave them permission to let go. Kirk had argued that the bold colors were tantamount to nature's use of color to draw attention for mating, but Brian had scoffed that his friend was watching too many late night Animal Planet specials.

"Strip." He heard her quick inhalation at his order and watched her eyes dart between the two of them before flickering briefly toward the door. "Regi, I gave you an order. You have two choices, comply or use your safe word." He'd teased her enough on the drive from the club that her slick little pussy had been aching for release, but he'd denied it by pulling back just before she'd been ready to orgasm—twice. The second time he'd actually heard her growl of frustration, so he knew her body was still craving the release. He really hadn't taken much of a gamble because she was already beginning to tremble in anticipation.

Brian had expected her to untie the small knot at the back of her neck and let the light green cotton dress slide to the floor, but she surprised him by reaching slowly for the hem of the short skirt. Crossing her arms as she slid her palms over her soft curves she grasped the hemline and pulled it over her head in a move that was pure seduction. He'd seen her naked before, but looking at her now— standing at the edge of their kitchen, completely bared to his gaze—was like seeing her for the first time. She was pure perfection and he heard Kirk's soft, "Beautiful" and couldn't have agreed more.

"She is stunning, isn't she? And she is all ours, aren't you, baby?" He didn't wait for her reply. Brian stepped to Regi's other side and skimmed his hand reverently down her bare back. Chill bumps followed his touch reassuring him that she was responding perfectly. "All that soft silky skin is ours to touch and mark. Seeing those dusty rose nipples pucker and tighten as they beg for our attention makes me anxious to see them in the new clamps we have for her. I can hardly wait to give her all the pleasure she deserves, but we need to get this punishment out of the way first."

"Tell us why you are being punished, *muñeca*." Kirk's voice was rough and Brian knew his friend was fighting the same urge to throw the entire plan out the nearest window and just fuck her on the nearest flat surface until none of them had any energy left.

Regi straightened her spine and then met his gaze as she answered. "I copped an attitude when you asked me when I'd last had a physical instead of just answering honestly."

Gotta give the woman credit for owning her mistakes and not being afraid to admit when she's fucked up.

"It isn't just that and I think you know it. Tell me what you think is at the crux of this issue." Brian knew his friend well enough to see Kirk was sure Regi understood exactly what he meant and they were even more convinced when they saw her swallowing down her gulp of surprise. She probably hadn't expected them to make her own-up to their real concern just yet. But since this was, in essence, one of the biggest issues they would have to tackle with her, they were simply going to begin as they intended to go. It had always been their guiding principle with subs and, dealing with the one they wanted to claim as their own, made the missive even more important.

This time her answer wasn't spoken with the same forcefulness and she was having trouble maintaining eye contact so Kirk used two fingers under her chin to force her eyes back to his. "Well, I guess I haven't really been taking very good care of myself and umm…well, I know that Doms get really pissy about that. Well, at least that is what some of the other subs have told me."

Brian held back his chuckle at her use of the word "pissy" because he didn't doubt for a moment who she'd quoted or that it was exactly the word Tobi West had used. Kyle and Kent had told him they didn't expect their sweet sub to be caught up on the punishments anytime soon. They'd stopped spanking her when they'd first found out she was pregnant despite his and Kirk's insistence that she'd be fine as long as they used common sense. But like most expectant fathers they'd coddled her until she'd dragged them both into their clinic and tearfully begged him to get them to back off. Brian really was fond of the little minx, but God in heaven the woman was going to lead every sub in the club into trouble. *More likely she'll rally the troops and lead a rebellion to take over the place.*

Brian stepped up to flank Kirk and nodded, "That's right and since this is an important lesson we're going to make sure it's one you don't forget." The flare of rebellion in her eyes was laced with just a bit of trepidation telling him she understood exactly what he was saying. This was not going to be an erotic spanking, she knew it and knew exactly what she'd done to earn it.

The purpose was to punish her for her lack of self-care, and he wasn't naïve enough to believe this was the only time they'd have to broach this subject. What she didn't realize was they were actually addressing something equally important. A Dom's most important obligations were to guide, direct, pleasure, and cherish. It was their job to provide her with what she needed even when she wasn't aware of the need or disagreed with their decision. It often took years to achieve the level of trust required for a submissive to surrender themselves to that level of control. But Regi was wound up like an eight-day clock and in need of a physical outlet for the negativity she was struggling so valiantly to control. Brian knew the next few minutes were going to be critical to whether or not their future included Regi, and he had no illusions about how easily it could all go wrong. However, he was also convinced the woman standing in front of him was worth the risk.

REGI'S HEAD WAS spinning and she felt like her heart was going to beat right out of her chest. This was one of the times she wished her brain had a switch that would let her just turn the damned thing off. She was just starting to wonder if they'd dimmed the lights when a heated slap to her bare ass caused her to gasp. Drown a damned duck, she'd been holding her breath. No wonder the room had started to dim. *Jesus Pete you are a dork, Regina. Way to blow your rep as an Ice Princess.* She'd heard the rumors and snarky whispers from club members who often felt she wasn't aware of her "place", which was a southern euphemism for being a bossy bitch. Hell *bitch* was one of the least offensive things she'd been called over the years. And she had always managed to smile politely even when she'd wanted to let the tears flow. There had been so many times she'd wanted people to know that she was just as vulnerable to their harsh words as any other submissive, but she'd known if she ever let anyone know there were cracks in the walls around her heart they'd find out just how fragile she really was. *Yeah, like I'm gonna let that happen.*

Her heart had leapt up into her throat when she'd heard the guys moving her things would be there soon. She'd known immediately that Brian and Kirk planned to include them somehow in her punishment, and *red* had been on the tip of her tongue until Brian had assured her Tank would not be coming upstairs. Her heart had warmed at his words, because he'd obviously taken care to consider her feelings. She'd seen other Doms exhibit similar regard for their subs and wondered what it would be like to have someone in your life that knew you well enough to anticipate your needs beyond their own next orgasm.

"Are you still with us?" In the back of her mind Regi heard a question, but hadn't tuned back in enough to register it had been directed toward her...until her left ass cheek felt like it had caught fire and a loud yelp escaped her lips before she could pull it back. *Holy fucking Hannah that hurt.* "Answer me, Regi. Are you ignoring my instruction or are we boring you to distraction?"

Like I'm going to answer a set-up question like that... Not! Reminds me of Tobi when she first got pregnant... She had come in to the Club's entry and asked if she looked pregnant or just fat. Oh yeah, talk about your classic lose-lose situation. This time her right cheek was blazing before she'd even registered the sound of the paddle whistling through the air. She'd yelped again, but this time it had been followed by a creative assessment of his mother's marital status when he was born.

"I'm not sure my mother will appreciate that comment, baby. And you have no one to blame but yourself, and just FYI, those will not count as swats for your punishment. Those were just to bring you back and get you focused on what we're doing here.

What? Those weren't gonna count? What the hell is wrong with him? I'll probably be black and blue for a week before this is done.

Chapter Eight

KIRK WATCHED AND listened as Regi fought the distraction that he suspected was often used as a way to stay disconnected. It was a habit he'd seen in other victims, if they didn't bond with anyone, the chances of getting hurt again were essentially eliminated. In Regi's case, her friendships at the club had already cracked the walls she'd erected. Now he and Brian needed to insert a few powerful explosives in those fissures and blow them completely apart.

She trembled as Brian bent her naked form over a bar stool he'd positioned at the edge of the living room so her bare ass and glistening pussy would be the first thing Dex and Ash saw when they stepped in the front door. That fact hadn't escaped Regi's attention either and he'd almost laughed when her nipples had drawn up to rock hard points as her eyes had darted to the door before draping herself over the stool.

God, the woman was so short they'd had to bring one of the spares they kept in a back closet because the stools the two of them used every day were too tall for her. To her credit she hadn't said anything about the fact her feet weren't anywhere near the floor when Brian had first directed her over the taller seat. Well, she hadn't said anything out loud, but he'd clearly heard her snarking questions about what did he expect and it not being her fault she wasn't a giant. Kirk had been forced to turn his back on her so she wouldn't see his smile, but as he'd been digging around in the toy bag he'd looked up to see her studying him in the reflection of the window. The ghost of a smile he saw on her face let him know he'd been busted, but she didn't mention it.

After she was secured over the lower stool, Kirk got a chance to see how dark red her ass was already from the two swats she'd already been given. Tracing his fingers over her skin, he looked at Brian with a raised brow. There were several vitamin deficiencies linked to a person bruising easily and he would bet a year's salary their sweet sub was skipping more than her share of meals because she was stashing every spare cent she earned. The battery of lab-work they'd be running for her would help identify exactly what was going on, but in the meantime they needed to dial back the intensity a few notches.

He leaned forward and pressed his lips against the bruised skin and felt her shiver. "We're going to have to be careful with you, *anoshi*. We'll talk later about how easily you are bruising, but for now I want to proceed so tell your Masters why you are being punished." She didn't hesitate to repeat their earlier conversation and she wisely dialed back the attitude. All the time she'd been answering, he'd been drawing his fingers through the slick folds of her sex. She was amazingly responsive, and when he'd circled her clit, he'd heard her whispered plea to heaven for help.

Stepping back so Brian could begin, Kirk moved to the door and opened it just as Dex and Ash stepped out of the elevator. Seeing the grim looks on their faces, he stepped into the foyer and started to pull the door closed behind him. Just as he pulled the heavy door forward the unmistakable sound of a wooden paddle connecting with bare skin was followed by Regi's gasp sent much of his blood racing south. The knowing look in their eyes told him both men had heard it as well. He gave them a quick update about the bruising and both men agreed to lighten up the swats they'd each give her.

Dex shook his head, "I can't say that I'm surprised, she didn't have shit in that dumpy kitchen. Well, unless you count the empty case of Ramen noodles in the trash. Christ, who knows how long she'd been eating that crap. There wasn't a fresh fruit or vegetable anywhere to be seen." Kirk remembered the Wests had been anxious for their former teammates to join the new team they were bringing together. From what he'd been told, aside from their obvious skills as operatives, both men were excellent cooks and nutrition conscious. When Gracie had been so ill at the beginning of her pregnancy, it had been Dex Raines who had continued to experiment with recipes until he'd hit upon several that had, according to Gracie, put him in line for sainthood.

Ash Moore leaned a shoulder against the wall giving Kirk a considering look. "Speaking of her apartment, Tank insisted that someone had been there after Regi would have left for work. Seems the Prairie Winds business manager is something of a perfectionist and honestly, we would have never noticed the things he pointed out as *out of place,* but he was convinced someone had been in her apartment." Kirk was a doctor, security wasn't his special-ty. But understanding what people were saying even when they weren't speaking was a central part of what he did every day and the two men standing in front of him were radiating tension and unspoken worry. "Listen, I know we said we'd bring her stuff here, but since there isn't much doubt that it's probably hot—umm sorry, bugged, we sent most of it out to Prairie Winds with Tank." Nodding to a small bag on the floor, he went on, "We pulled out just a few things we thought she might need until the rest can be cleared. And Tank wanted us to bring a small wooden box that he swears is her most treasured possession aside from the pendant she always wears. But even though the thing was really well hidden, we sent it with Tank."

Kirk knew there was more to the story because the tension was practically crackling off the two of them. And as an empath, Kirk was catching wave after wave of worry, but he wasn't able to hear their specific concerns. The realization that his connections with others were strengthening at a far slower rate than his link with Regi brought him up short. He promised himself he'd call his family soon, they deserved the courtesy of hearing about Regi from him, and until he could take her to meet them in person, it was the best he could do.

Dex shifted, drawing Kirk's attention back to the discussion. His distraction hadn't been missed and Kirk appreciated the fact neither man had commented on his lack of focus. "There is something else…the box? Tank said it was the only thing of her mother's that she managed to take from the boat, but I think it is more than just a small wooden box." Dex's glance moved to the door before returning to Kirk, "Let's get this over with and then we'll talk." Kirk nodded his agreement even though he was now mentally past the point he should be in order to follow through with what Regi really needed. She deserved his undivided attention and he wasn't certain he could do that when his worry for her safety had just been ratcheted up several notches by Dex's cryptic insinuation. *Damn soldiers and their non-speak. Just because they are accustomed to that less is more crap doesn't mean we all work that way. Fuck!*

REGI HEARD THE other men return to the room and if she hadn't been busy plotting ways to kill Brian Bennett she might have had the good sense to worry about her already throbbing backside. But as it turned out scheming a way to torture someone over a foot taller and outweighing her by God only new how much was using up all her brain cells that weren't busy chasing the release she had already been denied three times. Dr. No-Not-Yet was practically begging to be murdered if you asked her. Hell-fire, if she got an all-female jury she'd probably get some sort of award rather than a conviction. *Is there a Nobel Prize for world service by homicide? Well, if there isn't there should be. I wonder if they have a suggestion box on their web page. Something to check out. If I don't get to come soon I'm going to shatter into a zillion different pieces and then the damned family can just go piss up a rope.*

Kirk's warm palm traced up and down her spine, and even though he'd startled her at first his touch had been grounding. "*Anoshi*, what's got you so frustrated? There are many ways to punish a naughty sub you know." Regi didn't answer because she was trying hard to pull back the venomous response that had nearly escaped. This was not the time for transparency. Doms were always preaching how important it was for subs to be completely open and honest with their Dom and themselves. But Regi had seen it time and again, what they *meant* was they wanted her to tell them exactly what they wanted to hear…and to make them believe it was the truth.

A zing of heat went from her ass to her pussy before her mind had even registered what had happened. "I asked you a question and you know the rules, little sub." This time Kirk's words wafted over her ear in a warm rush of air that reinforced her feeling of vulnerability at the position she was in. *Question? He asked me a question?* "Do you need me to repeat the question, Regi?" *Well…yeah, but you called me by my name so that means I'm really in some serious trouble and I'm not sure I can cope with any more trouble at the moment…sort of maxed out on that…but thanks anyway.*

Dual snorts of laughter from her left reminded her that they weren't alone and she groaned when she realized she'd been speaking out loud. "I asked what had you so frustrated that you were plotting ways to get rid of one of your Masters, and I expect a truthful answer." Regi could hear the underlying amusement in Kirk's voice despite his efforts to play up his Dom role.

"He is torturing me, Sir." *See? I can be a good sub when I want to be. And I'm pretty sure I'm in deep enough already. I'll leave poking the bears to Tobi since she has that double cub insurance policy leading her everywhere she goes. Damn the woman looks like a fucking Weeble.*

This time it Dex's voice brought her back to the moment, "I do believe she is having trouble focusing on what's happening here. I'll bet we could find some great solutions to that if she wouldn't be sporting the evidence for the next week. Hell, I'll bet her ass would turn colors they haven't even dreamed up names for yet. But since she hasn't been taking very good care of this delicious little body, we'll have to make this short and sweet." He pushed her hair back out of her eyes and used his fingers to move her chin enough that her eyes met his, "But know this, sweetheart, if you were ours we'd beat your ass until you couldn't sit for a week for not taking care of yourself. The lack of anything nutritious in your apartment was appalling. You owe it to yourself and to everyone who cares about you to fix this, and we're all going to make sure you do exactly that." He pressed his lips gently against her forehead and then stood. Regi felt his two swats but knew he'd definitely not given her what he thought she deserved. She'd seen Dex and Ash in action and they were harsh…very harsh. It was a good thing the sub they'd been seeing was a pain-slut because there weren't many submissives at the club that were up to playing with these two.

The swats sent her arousal soaring again and she spent several seconds taking deep breaths and pulling herself back from the edge of release. Stealing an orgasm during a punishment, and before the Dom everyone claimed was a sadist had his turn, would not go well for her. When her breathing finally slowed she opened her eyes to see Ash Moore kneeling in front of her watching quietly. "I know how hard you worked to fight off that release, little one, and I'm proud of you. I think that I'm going to change what I had planned so you'll know how impressed I was with your effort." Regi's thoughts were still bouncing around enough that she wasn't sure whether he was being sarcastic or sincere, but in the end it wouldn't matter because they could and would do whatever they wanted to. "I'll only take one swat, but then I want the privilege of watching your Masters fuck you at the same time. You'll get your release after they've given their permission and not a moment before, do you understand?"

Understand? Is his kidding? Doesn't he hear the angel choir in the corner singing the Halleluiah Chorus? "Yes, Sir." *See? Perfect subbie answer, now let's get this show on the road before my body explodes from unfulfilled desire.* Ash's big SEAL paw landed and the burn was intense but manageable, but it insured she never wanted to be on the receiving end of a real punishment at his hand. She immediately heard the

79

unmistakable sound of a condom wrapper being ripped open just as Brian smoothed her hair back again and pressed the smooth head of his cock against her lips. Using her tongue to sample the pre-cum at the tip, the earthy taste was like a key unlocking her jaw and she opened wide and stretched forward until he was pressing against the back of her throat.

Regi heard Brian's sharp intake of breath just before his moan of pleasure. God it made her feel powerful to know she could have that kind of effect on him. But she didn't have long to languish in the tiny bit of control she'd managed to snag for herself, because Kirk slid through the swollen folds of her sex. He didn't stop until he was all the way in with his thighs pressed against her heated flesh and the tip of his cock pressed against her cervix. They didn't give her any time to collect her thoughts because they set a brutal pace from the very beginning. This wasn't about making love, this was about finally getting the relief they all three needed and barreling toward her like a tsunami wave.

Her entire body felt like it had been electrified, her muscles became rigid, and the walls of her pussy clamped down when Kirk's cock seemed to swell inside her. In the back of her mind she heard Brian and Kirk both growl for her to come with them, but she'd been holding back for so long she wasn't sure she could let go. But when Kirk reached around and pinched her throbbing clit between his fingers everything around her exploded in brilliant streaks of vibrating neon colors. She heard a woman screaming and men shouting and then her throat was being bathed in the hot jets of Brian's release. Regi managed to swallow down every drop of seed Brian gave her as Kirk pumped his release deep inside her. Even with the condom between them, she'd felt every pulse of warmth deep in her core.

Regi was barely cognizant enough to register the fact she'd been moved and Kirk carried her from the room. However, the tepid water from the shower was a shock to her sex warmed skin and she came wide-awake with a shriek. "Shhh. Settle, *mi amõre*. We'll take a quick shower and then our guests would like to speak with you." Kirk's large hands washed her quickly and efficiently, but his touch reignited her libido even though his motions weren't intentionally sensual. *What is it about these two that reaches into the very heart and soul of me?*

By the time she followed him back down the hall he'd combed out her hair and pulled it back into a loose braid. He'd given her one of his white dress shirts to wear, but the fact he'd only let her fasten two of the middle buttons and the transparency of the fabric meant his gesture hadn't been meant to conceal her from anyone's view. Now that her brain was starting to function again, she didn't doubt the move was intentional on several levels.

Walking in to the kitchen, Regi's stomach growled loudly at the rich aromas that filled the air. Brian had obviously taken his own shower, but was now setting plates and silverware on the counter. *Good Lord I just ate a little while ago, how can I possibly be hungry again?* But the smell of oregano was like a drug pulling her in. When Dex looked up from the sauce he was stirring his smile lit up his entire face and Regi was reminded why the other subs always referred to him as "the pretty boy Dom".

"Have a seat, Regi, we're just finishing up. We'll chat over dinner, such as it is." Regi didn't even realize she was staring at the bubbling sauce until he chuckled. "Go on now, sit down and sip your wine." Kirk's large hand encircled her wrist and with a gentle tug led her to the bar.

Lifting her onto the stool, he tapped the inside of her knee reminding her to part her legs. When she complied he nodded his approval and then sat beside her as Brian took the seat on her other side.

Watching the two former SEALs put the finishing touches on the meal they'd managed to pull together in a remarkably short amount of time reminded Regi of the Broadway shows her parents had taken her to as a child. Their movements were graceful and fluid, and they worked together with a well-choreographed ease that let her know they'd worked together for a long time. She'd dug in to the plate Ash set before her and moaned at the first bite. *Oh my God in heaven, I could die a happy woman after I finish this, but please if you really love me, God, you'll let me eat the entire thing first.*

When she finally looked up, all four men were staring at her, looks of astonishment on each of their faces. "What?"

Ash Moore's laughter broke their silence, "I swear if I ever find a woman that looks at me the way you looked at that pasta, I'm marrying her on the spot."

"And I hope she has your appetite, too, sweetheart, because watching you enjoy that was one of the sexiest things I've ever seen." Dex's words brought growls from the men flanking her, but she knew they were meant to take the sting out of the fact they'd been staring at her while she had practically inhaled her meal. "Of course she's going to have to enjoy pain a whole lot more than you do, but for now the honors for most lustful eating go to you."

Regi couldn't help but laugh at their teasing. She was grateful they'd dispelled any awkwardness that might have followed the earlier scene. Once they'd all finished eating and settled in the living room, Dex leaned forward with his elbows resting on his knees and gave her a considering look. "As I'm sure you know, Tank went with us to your apartment." When she nodded, he continued, "He pointed out several things that were out of place, things Ash and I wouldn't have ever noticed because they were so small. But Tank knows how meticulous you are and he spotted the inconsistencies right away, so instead of bringing your things here, we've sent most of them to Prairie Winds."

She must have looked alarmed because Dex quickly added, "We had a portable jammer and sent it with Tank. And of course as soon as he got close to Micah's Magic Show workshop everything would have fallen under his cloak of invisibility." Regi knew Micah had converted one of the old sheds on the grounds into a workshop he used for all his electronic gadgetry. Even after Micah, Jax, and Gracie moved into their new place next to Prairie Winds, he'd left the shop in place for the projects that held any potential hazards. One of the things Regi had learned quickly after starting her job at the club was that former SEALs loved anything they could blow up.

Ash cleared his throat to get her attention and asked, "Have you ever heard of Makishi puzzle boxes?" When she shook her head, he smiled. "Well I'm kind of a gadget guy and one of the things I'm pretty good at is puzzles. I think that small wooden box of your mom's is actually a Makishi. The top looks like a small jewelry box, but the bottom is false." Regi knew he'd paused to give her a chance to consider what he'd said and even though she was surprised at first, things started to slide into place pretty quickly.

"My dad was a big fan of puzzles...anything that re- quired him to think through a solution was great fun as far as he was concerned. It drove my mother to distraction. He'd hide her gifts and give her a treasure map with riddles or puzzles to solve. He almost always had given in, because despite the fact she was a gifted mathematician, she rarely managed to figure out all of his obscure clues. He was brilliant, really."

Sitting between Kirk and Brian was grounding her and for the first time since she'd lost her parents she was able to talk about them openly, and she could already feel her heart starting to mend. Kirk leaned forward directing his question to Dex, "Do you think you can open the box?" Dex's grin was answer enough and Ash's snort of laughter confirmed it.

"Yeah, but I wanted Regi's permission. I don't know how long it will take me to figure it out, but if your memory of the timeline the day your parents were killed is right, I suspect it won't be too difficult." Regi didn't understand how he'd drawn that conclusion and it must have shown in her face. "You said your mom went down-stairs to put away something she was holding in her hand. So it must have been small and I'm assuming she was going to hide it. The logical place for her to hide something that would fit in the palm of her hand would have been the box. Since it doesn't sound like she had a lot of time, I'm guessing it's fairly easy to access.

Regi felt like her world was tilting as if everything was trying to come into alignment, but wasn't quite there yet. It was discomforting even though she knew it would eventually bring her the peace of knowing why things had gone wrong so quickly that day. She didn't hesitate to give her permission and she felt chill bumps race up her arms as the last words her dad spoke to her whispered through her mind...*follow your heart, it will lead you to unimaginable treasures.*

Chapter Nine

C HARLIE HENDRICKS LEANED back in his leather office chair and wished he could take comfort in its familiar squeak, but time was quickly running out and he knew there wasn't going to be much comfort in his immediate future. He'd lived alone for so long, talking to people outside his ever-shrinking circle of acquaintances was rarely an occasion to celebrate—and today hadn't been any exception. The first call had been from his oncologist and the news had been exactly what he'd expected and everything he'd dreaded. His service to his country in Vietnam had exposed him to some of the most powerful carcinogens ever turned loose on mankind and even though they hadn't reared their ugly heads until decades later, when they roared to life a few years ago they had done so with a vengeance. The devastation the various cancers had wrought on his body made the man who greeted him each morning in the mirror a virtual stranger. But now that Dr. Doom and Gloom had assured him the end was near, Charlie didn't expect to see that stranger much longer. Like so many of his fellow patients, the only part of that he found frightening was the process, not the result.

The irony of the second call wasn't lost on him. One of the few contacts Charlie still had with the agency he'd dedicated the second part of his life to had called not an hour later, and his news had been even grimmer. He'd covered his tracks for many years and in today's world of instant information access that was damned impressive, but "the family" that had been looking for Regina for the past decade had finally tracked him down.

It had always amazed Charlie that a group of criminals as well organized as the Stephano family ordinarily was, had for all intents just accepted the "official version" of the story of Regina's disappearance. Of course he had never expected Mark to stay away from his daughter for so many years either, so what the hell did he know? The family matriarch had fallen ill not long after her granddaughter disappeared. Her slow slide into the darkness of dementia had been a closely guarded secret. Others in the family simply hadn't cared enough to investigate. They had simply assumed she was living in hiding and under a totally new identity, when in fact she had always been essentially hiding in plain sight.

He was the only person who had ever known exactly where she was or had the details of what she was still unwittingly holding. The truth of it was she would have been incredibly easy to find if they'd ever made a sincere effort. Charlie had instinctively known that Regina was safer just below the surface than she would have been buried deep. *The family* that wanted to reel her in was well connected to the underground scourge, but they had fewer connections among the average working class. Drug kingpins and sex slave traders didn't usually travel in working class social circles.

The bond between them had formed the instant the frightened young woman had run into his arms. Why she had instinctively trusted him was a question he'd asked himself hundreds of times over the past decade. He'd been on vacation in the western Caribbean when he'd gotten the call telling him to secure the boat and the girl. The minute he'd boarded he'd known things were not what they appeared to be and certainly not what someone wanted the terrified young woman on board to believe. The story had almost erupted from her and Charlie had never questioned her honesty, but he'd always known she'd been played…big time. What he hadn't known until a few weeks later was why.

Charlie rested his elbows on the chair's well-worn arm-rests, steepling his fingers, letting his thoughts drift. The phone call a few months ago from that former SEAL in Texas had seemed to set things in motion, and who was he to question the Universe's timing. Micah Drake had explained his position at the Masters of the Prairie Winds Club and Charlie had listened patiently as the man explained his observations and worry about his friend and co-worker.

As a former agent, he had been impressed the man had found him and even more impressed with how much Drake had already known about Regina, it was obvious his connections ran deep. Charlie hadn't given him any additional information because, in truth, there wasn't much more that would have addressed his concerns. The only other piece of information he had was the ace he'd held back all these years. He had wanted to keep Regina safe for as long as possible, and she'd been safer not knowing the power she held—but that had all changed now. As he picked up the phone and dialed the number Mr. Drake had given him, he hoped her friends and coworkers would help her because, quite frankly, he was getting ready to turn her world upside down. And his biggest regret was that he knew he wouldn't be there to help her through it.

REACHING OVER TO disconnect the call, Kyle West looked at the other men in the room and saw faces filled with concern that probably mirrored his own. When the former agent had first called him yesterday, Kyle had been surprised at the request for an emergency conference call that would include the club's entire security team and Regi. But now he understood the man's concern. If Hendricks was right, Regi could well be holding the keys to an almost unimaginable fortune. The implications were staggering, but it was the woman sitting in front of him that was his chief concern. She sat stone still in front of him, flanked by both Brian and Kirk. She hadn't spoken or so much as moved a muscle, but then neither had anyone else in the room.

For once, Kyle was grateful for his wife's irreverence because her low whistle from the back of the room was what broke the eerie silence. "Woah. The places my head is going with this information is scary...even for me and that's saying a lot." Kyle had asked Tobi to join them because he'd worried her friend might need the extra support and she'd readily agreed. She also had a razor sharp mind that processed information at lightning speed, and that was a bonus as well.

He'd loved their brainstorming sessions when the three of them had worked with the other Prairie Winds staff on the Forum Shops addition because Tobi didn't hold back when an idea came to her, she quickly tossed them out for the others to consider. When he'd commented on that one evening, citing how much he appreciated she was never offended when one of her ideas was rejected, she'd been confused. *'Why would I be offended? I throw everything out there and even if I don't come up with the solution, explaining why my answer won't work might lead somebody to an idea that will.'* It seemed to him that her interactions with people often came from that same place. She threw herself into relationships with everything she had and let the other person decide how much to accept.

Tobi moved to the front of the room and tried to perch herself on the corner of Kyle's desk, but couldn't hoist her rounded-self high enough. "That's it...I'm officially rounder than I am tall. Damn this bites. It just frosts my cookies I tell you. You'd think my obstetricians would take pity on me and pry the little brats out of there...hell, use a crowbar if you have to. But damn and double damn this is just getting old." Kent moved a cushioned chair behind her and steadied her as she lowered on to it. "Don't go away, husband mine, because I'll need you to run the crane to get me back up."

Kent leaned forward and kissed her with unrestrained passion and then grinned, "Remember, we promised you we'd always be here to catch you, and that includes helping you back to your feet, sweetness." Kyle watched the interplay between the two most important people in his life and smiled. It wouldn't be long until their family expanded by two and he wasn't sure who more anxious, Tobi or his mom, or perhaps they were equally invested in seeing the pregnancy end, but for different reasons.

TOBI TRIED TO lean forward to grasp Regi's hands and finally gave up, exclaiming, "This is just crazy. I can't even reach over them anymore." Regi heard the desperation in her friend's voice, scooted her chair to Tobi's side, and grasped her hand. Regi didn't think Tobi had even realized she was crying until Regi dabbed her eyes with the soft handkerchief Kyle had handed her. Her bosses had told her several weeks ago they'd started carrying them because Tobi had become so emotional it seemed as though they were always searching for tissues to dry her tears.

"You know, Lilly tells me that as soon as these babies are born everyone will focus on them and I'll feel left out. But I don't think I'll feel left out at all, I'll just be happy to stop leaking." Glancing around the room at the men whose expressions ranged from curious confusion to horror, Tobi burst out laughing. "Damn, sorry about that, guys. Guess that was a bit more information than you all needed, huh?" Regi chuckled at her friend and grateful for the distraction because it had given her a couple of minutes to regroup.

Tobi straightened and Regi noticed her wince but Tobi waved off her concerned look. "I'm fine. First things first. You gave Ash permission to figure out the puzzle box, right?"

"Absolutely. I was never any good at that sort of thing and I'd probably get tired of trying and destroy it with a big hammer." Regi felt Kirk step up behind her and place his hand over her shoulder. It surprised her how much that simple gesture calmed her. *Didn't she hear him say something about his grandmother being a healer? I wonder if that's a genetic trait.*

Kirk's words warmed her ear, "It is. And I'm anxious for you to meet her, *anoshi*." When he returned to his seat he asked, "What do you think of Mr. Hendricks' suggestion that you might be holding some kind of map? Had your parents given you any indication that this salvage operation was any different than the others they'd done?"

Regi considered the questions for a few seconds before shaking her head, "I'm not saying he is wrong, but I don't have any reason to think he is right either. Although I have to admit, a couple of things stand out about that day, now that I think about it. I just wish I could have seen more…but those damned louvers kept me from seeing everything clearly." She took a deep breath squaring her shoulders and decided to just spit it all out. "First, my dad never took off the Hunab Ku pendant he'd found on a salvage they'd done earlier in the year. I wasn't along on that trip, they'd arranged for me to travel with a friend and her family while they did that one. When I asked about the pendant, he told me it held all the answers to the future. I thought he was talking about universal knowledge because I'd been taught about the Mayan belief that the universe is controlled by mathematical laws, and that it is those laws that lead to higher levels of awareness and consciousness. I didn't question him, but I did notice he kept that pendant on *all the time*, even when he was diving and having something around your neck was something he'd always strictly forbidden. But you know, I was fifteen…looking forward to being sixteen in a few days. I was focused on the party they'd promised me and hadn't considered it worth questioning. I just wanted to get through the last couple of dives and get back to shore."

As Regi had been speaking, she'd noticed that Brian was focused on her, but Kirk seemed to be watching Tobi. She'd felt Tobi shift several times but assumed her discomfort was a result of sitting in one position for too long, something she'd heard her friend curse about for the last few months. She heard Tobi moan softly just before she gasped, and suddenly Regi felt like she was watching a scene from a comedy play out in slow motion around her.

Kirk was kneeling in front of Tobi with his palms bracketing her rounded belly speaking to her and glancing at his watch. Brian picked Regi up and moved her to the side just as Kent and Kyle West leapt to Tobi's side. Just as her feet hit the floor, she heard four different phones chime and watched as Jax, Micah, Brian, and Kirk all pulled out their phones.

Jax and Micah sprinted in from the room just as Brian leaned down and whispered in her ear, "I would have bet my interest in heaven Gracie and Tobi would do this." She must have looked confused because he kissed her temple then chuckled, "Gracie's water just broke. Lilly was with her and Tobi is also in labor. If I was betting, I'd say she probably has been in labor most of the morning, but she wasn't planning to say anything until after this meeting—something that is going to cost her dearly when her men get wind of it."

REGI HADN'T EVER seen Brian and Kirk in "professional" mode, but standing near the door of the waiting room that was quickly filling to capacity afforded her a view of the nurses station and hallway so she'd been able to watch them as they interacted with the staff and four frenzied fathers-to-be with seamless grace. Even though she was too far to hear most of what they were saying, their body language radiated a calm confidence despite the whirling chaos that surrounded them. As she was admiring their self-assuredness, she found herself smiling. *Holy hell they are just fucking hot. And who knew that scrubs could be sexy?* A split second after the thoughts went through her mind, her body responded. Her nipples were suddenly tight enough the lace of her bra was chafing their tips and her pussy was wet and the tissues already swelling enough that she unconsciously shifted to ease the pressure on her clit. As if on cue Kirk looked up from the chart he'd been writing in and met her gaze, a slow knowing smile lit up his face. Kirk leaned over and whispered to Brian, and his eyes zeroed in on her with the pinpoint accuracy of a laser beam. His raised brow told her he knew exactly why she was shifting from foot to foot, and when he playfully shook his finger at her she froze. She felt like a child caught with their hand in the cookie jar and wasn't even sure why. Well, that wasn't entirely true, she had worked at the club long enough and read enough about D/s relationships to know subs weren't allowed to get themselves off. All of their pleasure belongs to their Dom, and he or she decides if—when—how. And as Hattie always said, *isn't that a fine how-do-ya-do?* Because she'd been so young, the elderly housemother for the small dorm Regi lived in while she was in college had taken Regi under her wing. Hattie had been a lifesaver during those first years after she'd lost her parents. And Regi knew the sweet grandmother had held off retiring until Regi had graduated. *God I miss her, she and Charlie were the only reasons I didn't drown in grief.*

Regi looked up to see both Kirk and Brian stalking toward her. Her entire body felt like it was lighting up from the inside out and the only thought her mind could manage was…*Mine!* Kirk reached her first and leaned down to whisper against her ear, "I do love seeing you lost in desire, *anoshi*. And I promise you we will fuck you before we all leave this hospital because there is no way we'd make it home. You just keep thinking about what it's going to feel like to be pinned against a door with my cock hammering into your depths until you're mind fractures, sending splintered pieces into space when you come around me."

She knew her breathing had sped up and damn it now she'd get to spend the rest of the day in wet panties. "But first, I've got a patient who is ready to bring twins in to this world so I need to go. Be a good girl and stick close to the others so you are safe." With that he turned and walked back the way he'd come.

Brian brushed his fingertips along the underside of her chin. She turned to see his blue eyes dark with desire and something else that she wasn't sure she was ready to name just yet. "Baby, your need is written all over your face and I promise you we'll take care of that before we leave the hospital—and probably several more times after we get you home. There are some very creative possibilities running through my head and I can hardly wait to see which of those play out later. But right now, your sweet friend, Gracie, needs some help getting that ornery baby of hers to make a debut. And she deserves all of my attention, so you stay with the others who are waiting and stay safe. Trust me, we'll be back just as soon as we can. Bringing new life into this world always jazzes us, and losing ourselves in your sweet body will be the perfect way to enjoy the high."

The soft kiss Brian brushed over her lips was just enough to throw a little gas on the fire and Regi felt her body respond with another surge of desire. *Damn men anyway, wind me up and then leave me.*

Chapter Ten

TOBI WEST LOOKED between her two husbands and snarled. For just a brief moment she wondered if that animalistic noise had actually come from her, but the looks on their faces confirmed it had indeed. It wasn't the first time Kirk had heard a woman in labor make a sound he'd found a little too close to demonic for his comfort, but it was the first time he'd heard it from a woman he considered a close personal friend. He looked up from checking on his patient's progress to see stricken looks on both Kyle and Kent West's faces and had to hold back his laughter. *Use your head, Tobi. Now is the time to negotiate your way out of all those punishments you've earned over the past eight and a half months.*

"Kitten, are you sure you are alright? I don't think I've ever heard anything quite like that before." Kyle's question earned him a glare from Tobi so intense Kirk expected to see her head start spinning around on her slender neck.

"No I'm not alright, Kyle West. Do I look alright? Are you insane? Kirk isn't giving me any good drugs and the asshat had the audacity to say it was my own fault for waiting so long to come to the hospital. That information would have been valuable ahead of time. It wasn't in that lame-assed pamphlet he gave me…I'm just sure it wasn't. That isn't a detail I'd forget. I don't like pain. I would have remembered any time issues related to pain relief. Fuck me. No on second thought—don't'. That's what got me into this mess." Even though he was sitting on a stool between the stirrups her feet rested in, Kirk wasn't about to take issue with being called an asshat. *Every obstetrician knows there are times when it is not wise to draw attention to yourself—and this was definitely one of those moments.*

"It'll all be over soon, sweetness. And then you'll have two babies to help you forget this part." And then Kent further submarined himself by adding, "I read that in one of the books." *Oh brother, the man couldn't have painted a larger target on himself if he'd tried.*

As expected, Tobi turned on him like a viper. "And do you know where you're going to find that book, Kent? We'll see how inclined you are to be comforted by my patronizing assurances that pushing the book out of one of your body's orifices will be *over soon*. Over soon...over soon, my ass. What did you two put in me any-way...elephants?"

Kirk almost cringed and sent up a silent prayer that Kent wouldn't take the bait, but when he saw his friend grin, he knew it had been in vain. "Oh yeah, baby...wanna see the daddy elephant's trunk?" *Oh shit, we may have to sedate Tobi and probably a couple of the nurses in the room.*

"Mr. West, could I see you for a moment, please?" Laughing to himself, Kirk watched one of his favorite nurses escort Kent out into the hall. When the alarm on Tobi's blood pressure monitor sounded, another nurse moved into Kent's place and gestured to Kyle to join his brother. *Fuck, this is going to get ugly if I don't do something.*

"Tobi, we're making great progress, but I think a change of scenery might help kick things up a bit. What do you say I let Lilly and Regi pop in for a minute?" At the very least, the other two women would be able to distract

Tobi enough to help her through the next phase of labor and the nurses should have her husbands lined out by the time the finale rolled around. Tobi tearfully agreed and Kirk made a quick trip to the waiting room for back up.

BRIAN BENNETT WATCHED Gracie let go of Jax McDonald's hand long enough to sign frantically. When Gracie's other husband, Micah Drake, looked at Jax in question, Jax's voice reflected the tension they were all feeling, "She just used every sign language curse I've ever seen and several new ones I'm not sure I want to know the meanings of." Things hadn't been going very well, Gracie's long struggle with nausea had taken a toll on her strength, and neither she nor the baby were holding up well under the strain of labor. She'd been cursing in Spanish until a few minutes ago and Brian had wondered why she'd bothered when everyone in the room spoke the language fluently. Although he had to admit, a few terms he'd assumed were a matter of regional dialect because he hadn't heard them before, but he'd been around enough women in labor to know better than to inquire.

Looking over the printouts from the monitors, Brian wasn't happy with the trend he was seeing. It was time to have a heart to heart with his friends and he wasn't looking forward to changing the way Gracie had seen this day playing out. He moved to stand alongside Micah and Gracie shifted her fatigue strained gaze to him. "Gracie, sweetheart, this isn't moving along fast enough and the strain has been causing a slow, but steady decline in both your and the baby's conditions. We can wait and watch things for a few more minutes or I can get things rolling for the C-section I'm sure we're facing. Do you have any questions before I step out of the room and give you and your husbands a chance to talk it over?"

Big tears filled her eyes quickly spilling over as she shook her head no, indicating she didn't have any questions. He and Kirk always prepared their patients for this possibility so it wasn't uncommon for them to already understand what they were facing, but he liked to give them a chance to address any concerns if it was at all possible. Jax surprised him by following him out into the hallway leaving Micah to comfort Gracie. "Get things in place, we all know this is the best option. How long until you're ready?"

Brian smiled and answered honestly, "Not long—ten minutes until everybody is in place because I'd actually alerted them a half hour ago this was probably coming. Better to call them in and then send them home than to need a team that isn't here. I won't have Kirk as secondary because he's busy trying to deliver Tobi's babies and keep Kent and Kyle from being lynched." Jax snorted a laugh even as he raised a brow in question. "I'll let them fill you in later, but suffice to say, I think we need to add a session on what to *not say* to your wife during labor to our maternity care."

REGI HAD BEEN pacing the hallway since she and Lilly had left Tobi's room. They'd both stared in disbelief as Tobi had vacillated between tears and rage while she'd recounted Kent's final indiscretion before the nurses had given both men a stern lecture on surviving the labor and delivery of their children. For a few seconds Regi hadn't been sure if Lilly was going to be able to remain calm, but the West family matriarch had given an Oscar-worthy performance. Tobi had been much calmer by the time they'd left her in her husbands' capable hands. Both men had returned to Tobi's room looking like they'd been through a battle of wills with the nurse and had immerged on the short end of the deal. Regi had been proud of herself for not cheering on the tiny medical whirlwind. The woman obviously cared deeply for her patients and wasn't impressed with either Kent or Kyle's size, wealth, or Dom-attitude.

Neither Tobi nor Gracie knew the sex of the babies they were carrying because their husbands hadn't wanted to know. It hadn't been a surprise to anyone that Tobi had been particularly vocal about her frustration with the men's decision. Tobi told her she'd thrown such a tantrum during her sonogram that Kirk had threatened to paddle her himself if she didn't settle down. Regi had finally given up holding back her roaring laughter when her friend admitted she'd been angry with her husbands and doctor, but she'd been infuriated by the fact she couldn't sit up by herself to rail at them.

Jax McDonald's worried expression when he stepped into the over-crowded waiting room brought Regi back to the moment. As she listened to Jax relay the reasons Gracie was being prepped for a C-section, she moved to his side and grasped his enormous hand in her own. He'd simply threaded their fingers together and held on, willingly accepting the gesture of friendship for the show of support it was. When he leaned down to give her a quick hug she'd told him, "I can hardly wait to hold your baby and give my friend a big hug of congratulations. You get out here as soon as you can and share your good news with us, okay?"

She'd deliberately kept her words positive and his smile told her how much he appreciated the gesture.

FOUR HOURS LATER, Brian and Kirk stood shoulder-to-shoulder and watched Regi shift nervously from foot to foot under their intense gaze. They had both successfully seen their respective patients through their deliveries and immediate aftercare. The babies and their mamas had made it through the initial wave of family and friends wanting their first looks at the still unnamed children. Now both mothers were finally resting peacefully while all four fathers wandered around with what the OB staff affectionately referred to as the "new parent glaze" in their eyes. A look they'd both seen hundreds of times, but it was such a contrast to the controlled expressions the four Masters usually displayed that even the two of them had shared a laugh about it. He and Kirk had both already hit the showers and were now back in their familiar jeans and boots.

Brian watched Regi's eyes trace their oxford shirts to where they were tucked in and he saw her pupils dilate when she took in the obvious bulges they were both sporting. They'd let her have her time with her friends, but they'd steered her into this small room the hospital administrators called an office even though in reality it was little more than a closet with a pressed wood desk and folding chair. When Regi licked her lips in nervous anticipation he was finished waiting, "Strip, baby. I think we are all ready for some much needed stress relief." When her hands began to slowly move to the hem of her shirt he was completely drawn in by her sensual striptease.

When she opened the front clasp of her bra and let the straps slide slowly down her arms baring high firm breasts with tightly peaked nipples, Brian heard Kirk's low whistle of appreciation. "Fuck me. You are stunning, *anoshi*. Even in this God awful florescent lighting, you take my breath away." Brian couldn't have agreed more and the only thing better than watching her, was running his fingers over all that satin-soft skin just before sliding into her wet heat.

"The rest of it. *Now*. And teasing your Masters is dangerous, sweetness. We love watching you, but there is a line between sensuality and teasing that you don't want to cross." The truth was there wasn't any such thing, and even if there was, the damned thing was a thousand miles from here. But his body was throbbing and the urge to shove her against the wall and just push his cock as deep into her as he could was growing with each panting breath he saw her take. The pulse at the base of her throat was framed by the gold chain holding the pendant he'd never seen her without, and watching her heartbeat's acceleration was pushing him dangerously close to the edge. As she slid the faded jeans and lace thong down her legs, Brian watched the pendant twist and swing. When she stood again, he noticed the gold piece her father had given her that fateful day was lying face down and he realized it was the first time he'd ever seen the back of the heavy piece.

Brian stepped forward and ran his finger down the chain to the disc it held and wondered if she'd ever given any thought to what the symbols on the back might mean. It was a question he planned to ask, but right now he had something much more personal in mind. "We have so many things planned for you, baby. But most of those will have to wait until we're home."

Kirk had stepped around behind Regi and Brian could

see his friend was trailing kisses from below her ear down her slender neck to the sensitive spot where her neck joined her shoulder. Brian watched Kirk open his mouth and he knew from the way her muscles turned to mush that he'd clamped his teeth over the spot they'd discovered could freeze the fiery woman in her tracks. Kirk's arm encircled her waist and probably the only thing keeping her on her feet. Brian leaned forward, licked a circle around one nipple, and then blew a puff of air over it watching it pull up even tighter. "I can hardly wait to clamp these beauties. And the emerald weights are going to drive you insane, love."

Rolling his tongue around the other bud and then sucking it in without mercy had her moaning loud enough to be heard by anyone walking down the busy hallway outside the door. Kirk released his mouth revealing the mark he'd left behind and admonished her, "Better keep quiet, *anoshi,* or you'll be explaining to some cranky charge nurse why you're seducing two of her favorite physicians in her office." Brian nearly laughed out loud at the strangled sound Regi made when she thought they'd taken over the nurse's office for this liaison. And while it was technically true that tonight's charge nurse often used this small space, it wasn't actually her office so the chances of her walking in on them were slim.

Brian kept up his ministrations to her perfect breasts until Kirk pulled her head back and turned her face to his, covering her mouth with his own in a kiss that was smoldering to watch. Once he knew her cries would be captured by Kirk, Brian moved to the junction of her thighs and slid his tongue into her wet folds. Her waxed pussy lips made her particularly sensitive and, at his first touch, her legs moved apart all on their own. "Such a good girl. So very responsive. But let's see how long you can hold back your release, shall we? Don't come until Master Kirk pinches those pretty nipples, that will be your signal to let go and fly for us." He didn't wait for her to agree, he just leaned forward pressing his tongue back into her sex and began lapping up all the sweet cream. She'd become so wet there were rivulets of her honey beginning to run down the inside of her thighs. He groaned against her swollen flesh and felt the vibrations move through the tissues just as she sagged completely in Kirk's arms. When he slid a finger into her tight sheath he felt the muscles of her vaginal walls rippling with almost seismic force. "Not yet, baby. If you come too soon, you'll be getting a spanking when we get home instead of the rewards we have planned for you."

"Oh...please. I can't hold on much longer. It's too good." Regi's words were filled with lust-filled desperation and Brian gave Kirk a quick nod. They launched an all-out assault on Regi's senses, Brian sucked her clit in and bit it lightly as he pumped two fingers in and out of her. He made sure the pads of his fingers pressed against the spongy spot at the front of her vagina that would send her into a rolling flash fire of an orgasm.

Kirk slammed his lips to hers and pinched both nipples at the same moment, rolling the taunt flesh between his fingers. Regi's entire body went rigid and in the next heartbeat Brian could hear the muffled scream that wasn't entirely contained. Her cream rushed over his fingers and the wet sounds of his fingers moving in her as he brought her down slowly had his cock threatening mutiny. When Kirk released her mouth Brian heard her gasps as she tried to fill her lungs with oxygen. He rose to his full height and waited until her eyes focused on his face before moving his drenched fingers up and sucking them into his own mouth so her essence coated his taste buds.

"Let's get her dressed and home. *Now.*" Kirk's vehemence surprised him because Brian was usually the more impatient of the two of them. But he wasn't about to argue the point. Their place was actually fairly close to the hospital, but that didn't mean they'd make it all the way upstairs before taking her. Suddenly elevator sex was sounding like an idea minted in gold.

Chapter Eleven

DEX RAINES HAD spent the better part of three days working on Regi's wooden puzzle box, so when it suddenly opened he could only stare at it in stunned silence for several seconds. Most of the boxes he'd worked to solve required at least twenty individual steps. And even though some of those steps were the same, just in different configurations, they still required individual movements. But nothing he'd tried had worked so he'd finally started working backward, subtracting a step each time from what was considered standard. Four had been the magic number. No doubt the box had been custom made to allow for quick access and that had answered some of the questions he'd had about the timeline of Regi's memory of that day on the boat.

He was sitting at a table in the club's main lounge and his gasp had gotten Kent West's attention. As one of the club's owners, Dex knew Kent had been checking the bar's inventory, but he was now looking up from the clipboard he'd been studying. Dex had to smile because his friend and boss looked like shit. For a man who had been through BUDs training, where functioning without sleep was a survival skill, Kent was certainly showing the strain of the sleep deprivation that accompanied new fatherhood.

"Did you get it open?" Kent's eyes had gone from weary to interested in a heartbeat when he'd glanced at the box lying open on the table. *Ahhh, nice to see the Special Forces operative I know is back.*

"Yeah, come over here and act as my witness if you have a minute." Dex didn't want there to ever be any question about what had been inside. He flipped open his phone and called Regi but his call was bounced to voicemail so he typed in a quick text before tossing his phone on to the table.

"Sure, any excuse to sit down for a few minutes has my name written all over it. Damn, who knew people so small could make so much noise. And sometimes the stench is enough to gag me." Kent was a large man and that made the shudder Dex saw race through him all the more amusing. "Sure you laugh now, but you'll see someday. And if you tell Tobi I said any of this I'll fire your ass and then tie some of those nasty diapers to you and toss you in the river. I'm sure those things must be able to take on a thousand times their own weight so you'll sink like a fucking rock." Dex couldn't hold back his howl of laughter and Kent's reluctant smile belied his words. "So, what's in the box?"

Dex pulled out the folded paper and spread it out on the table between them. "Looks like somebody added a note to the top of a sheet of code. Is that Morse?"

"I don't think so, doesn't look right but hell, what do I know. I can't even read the note at the top, although I do think it just might be English." Dex wasn't as convinced. He'd never seen writing quite that bad.

"Fuck it. I hope this makes more sense to Regi. Or maybe her men, hell, they're doctors. They are supposed to be known for their horrendous handwriting, aren't they?" Dex had no more than spoken the words when Kirk and Brian settled in to the two empty seats at the small table.

"I think I resent that remark. What about you, Kirk?" Brian was grinning as Kirk rolled his eyes. "Regi is on her way, she got your message. We were checking on the new mothers and she stayed upstairs to rock Kodi so Tobi could take a shower." Looking over at Kent, Brian grinned, "That little girl is gonna be a handful. Kameron was sleeping so soundly even his sister's wailing didn't rouse him." It amazed everyone how different the two were in temperament. Kodi was just like her mother, full of energy and vocal about everything. Her brother was more reserved and according to Tobi he had already perfected his fathers' *Dom-look*. Brian and Kirk had both laughed out loud when they'd heard Tobi cooing to him and warning him that his little Dom stare wasn't going to work on her any better than his daddies' did.

Dex slid the paper over in front of Brian and Kirk, then waited as they studied it. When he saw them both frown he knew they weren't having any more luck than he and Kent had. "Is that a flag symbol? And that looks like it might be a lower-case e. But after that I'm stumped."

Regi had walked up behind Kirk without any of them noticing and leaned over Kirk's shoulder and laughed. "My dad was always complaining to mom about her handwriting. He was particularly adverse to her habit of making rounded letters pointed. Like that, it isn't a flag, it's a capital p." Kirk pulled her around and settled her on his lap as she continued studying the paper. Dex smiled at Kirk's casual move and was grateful the two physicians seemed to be making progress with the club's spirited office manager.

WHEN REGI FIRST looked at the paper spread out in the middle of the table her heart had stuttered. Just seeing something her mom had written had stolen her breath for a few seconds. But she'd forgotten her trepidation quickly as she'd studied the writing in the top margin. The bottom of the note was easy, it was a series of Mayan numbers. And if Regi was to guess, she'd bet it was the location of the last salvage they'd been on. She remembered her dad had always rolled his eyes about his wife's obsession with numbers. He'd dictate the GPS coordinates to her and she'd translate them into any one of several ancient number systems as a way to *code* the information. He'd always laughed because there was rarely anyone within miles of them, and he'd teased her about missing her calling as a super-spy in antiquities espionage.

What puzzled Regi was the fact her mom had evidently been concerned enough about the speedboats that had been closing in on them that she'd taken the time to scribble a note at the top of the sheet of numbers. *No surprise there. Mom loved number games and she would have known no one would know what she'd done.* When Regi had been younger, her Dad had been the one who had coded information, but her mom had teased him so mercilessly about his attempts he'd turned the task over to her. And even though she'd teased him about being overly paranoid about his family, she'd quickly made a game out of the task.

"*Anoshi,* can you make any sense of this?" Kirk's words were spoken in a warm wash over her ear, but loud enough for the others sitting around the small table to hear. She looked up from the paper to see the other three men were looking at her rather than the paper they'd been studying so intently just minutes before.

Regi had trouble suppressing her smile, it was a part of her life that no one at Prairie Winds knew anything about. She'd actually been surprised when the Wests had hired her without questioning the fact she had majored in Antiquities, instead they'd focused on her minor in Business and she'd been happy to let them. Only in the past few days she'd learned her bosses had known about her past and had contacted Charlie several times over the years…something she planned to take up with her friend and mentor during their next video call.

Scrambling off Kirk's lap, Regi stepped behind the bar to find paper and a pencil. When she started to pull another chair up to the table Kirk shackled her wrist with his large hand and shook his head as he pulled her back to his lap. "I don't think so, *mi amõre*." Regi tried to ignore the fact Kirk had immediately pulled her knees apart and Brian's fingers were tracing slow circles along the inside of her thigh as she focused on the strange symbols and numerals at the bottom of the paper.

"I think these are intended to be the longitude and latitude of the wreck we were working on, but I know they arcn't right. I don't remember the exact coordinates, but these are definitely wrong." And she suspected they were off by specific and varying amounts, just because that would be so typical of how her mom's mathematician's mind had always done things. Using her pencil to retrace her mother's writing at the top of the paper, Regi couldn't hold back her smile. "Now, *this* I can read, but it doesn't make any sense."

When she looked up, Kyle had joined them. He was standing between his brother and Dex and he was looking directly at her. "Explain."

Regi grinned at his one-word command. She was accustomed to his brusque communication style so his comment didn't bother her. "What you thought was a flag is a capital P. Dad was always complaining about Mom's habit of making straight lines for the rounded parts of letters...it drove him crazy for some reason, and I'm sure that was a large part of why she did it. They had the best marriage...so in love and willing to battle against both of their families' objections to make their own way." Even she had been able to hear the whimsical tone her voice had taken on as she'd lost herself in the memories for a few seconds.

She heard the groans from around the table and Kyle's soft curse, "I swear to all that is holy Tobi is contagious." Regi started to protest but the look on his face and Brian's pinch to the inside of her thigh made her reconsider the wisdom of what she'd been planning to say. *No reason to get myself into a pickle when I'm so outnumbered...that is just bad planning.* She started to laugh at her own nonsense, but was sure they'd take it as a personal affront so she just went back to what she was sure her mom had intended as a clue.

"Anyway, the word is 'Pend'. I know the end looks like 'c l', but I'm sure it is a 'd', even though I have no idea what it means." She heard Brian's soft gasp from beside her and turned to him in question.

"Baby, take off the pendant your dad gave you." She blinked at him several times in confusion, but when it became clear he hadn't been kidding, she reluctantly pulled her most treasured possession over her head and handed it to him. Watching as he turned it over, she bent over to look at the symbols he was pointing to. "I noticed the back of the pendant a few days ago and had intended to ask you what these meant, but to be honest, I'd just simply forgotten until now."

It was as if something shifted inside her mind and the events of that day started to swirl though her thoughts at such a dizzying speed that Regi slid her hands to the edges of the table as if gripping it would keep her from getting pulled into the vortex of the whirlwind surrounding her. There were so many loose threads over the years and each time she'd ask Charlie for clarification, he'd reminded her that *everything is revealed when the heart is ready*. More than once she had wanted to reach through the phone and slap him for his lame answer. Was it possible that she was finally ready to fully understand what had happened that day?

She knew her memory had holes in it, there wasn't any way someone could remember each and every detail of a traumatic event. When the counselors she visited in the beginning failed to provide the answers she'd sought, Regi had taken it upon herself to study the effects of fear on eyewitnesses' testimony. The more she'd learned, the more questions she'd had about that day. Looking between the former Special Forces operatives seated around her, Regi asked, "Do you know a cryptologist that you trust implicitly?"

Kyle and Kent both raised brows in mirrored moves that she might have found amusing any other day. None of them said anything for several seconds—as if they were waiting for her to continue so she reluctantly added, "There was more to my dad than anyone knew…his family was…well, something of a continuing *issue*."

"The short answer to your question is *yes*, we do know someone we'd trust. Hell, we've all put our lives in his hands more than once. But quite frankly I'm not inclined to bring anybody else in to this without knowing more about what we're up against." Kyle ran his hands through his hair and turned to Micah. "Why don't you tell Regi what we know and then let's go from there."

Before Micah could begin, Dean and Dell West sauntered in the back door and pulled up chairs behind Kent. The fact they'd chosen a position that put them in her line of sight wasn't lost on her. Dean winked at her, "Darlin' we got wind of this little pow-wow and thought maybe you could use a couple of extra fellas on your side."

Dell grinned, "Not that our sons and their pals here *aren't* but sometimes they focus so much on the forest that they forget about the value of taking care of each individual tree, and that is where we'll come in. And you never know when our resources might come in handy." Regi loved Kent and Kyle's fathers. She loved Lilly as well, but Dean and Dell had always reminded her of the special bond she'd shared with her dad, and she'd felt drawn to them from the first time they'd met. She grinned at the two older men and then returned her attention to Micah.

For the next thirty minutes, Regi listened as Micah Drake recounted everything they knew about her family and their various *business interests*. Obviously all of her attempts to keep her past under wraps had been a wasted effort and she wondered again why she'd bothered. How had she believed she could keep anything from men with their training and connections? It was humbling to find out they actually knew more about her parents than she did. Because even though she had suspected her father was more than just a treasure hunter, she'd never had any way to confirm her suspicions. In the beginning she'd just seen Charlie's ability to wade through paperwork as a blessing, but eventually she'd begun wondering how he'd been able to effortlessly manage all of the shortcuts he'd found. It had always seemed odd that a covert agent had just happened to be vacationing in the area and had willingly taken her under his wing, but she'd never wanted to delve too deeply into what had clearly worked in her favor.

While Micah had been speaking, Regi had noticed Kyle stepping away from the group to speak on the phone. Looking up at him when he returned, she saw him grin as he shrugged, "We didn't say the expert was far away. Carl Phillips has hidden talents."

"Besides moonlighting for Nascar?" Regi had heard Jen recount the story of Carl's driving antics. Jen had sworn she hadn't been sure she was safer in a truck with Carl behind the wheel or with the kidnappers that had been holding her in the American Embassy in Bolivia.

"I'm going to have to talk to Jen's Masters about her tendency to exaggerate." Carl's quiet voice sounded right behind her and Regi nearly jumped off Kirk's lap. All the men sitting around the table laughed as Regi spent several seconds trying to calm her racing heart.

"It's not nice to sneak up on people, soldier boy. Damn it, I'm going to get one of those rearview mirror headsets that cyclists wear. Or maybe I'll just tie bells to each of you. Yeah, that's it...I can let the clanging of the bells trumpet your approach. Holy hand-puppets, I'll bet I can get a cardiologist to agree that my heart needs the break." One of the first things Regi had learned when she'd started working for the Wests was that Special Forces operatives moved with amazing stealth. How men that large were able to move in almost complete silence was still a mystery to her. "You know it really isn't fair at all. You all are enormous and yet you move like ghosts. And Tobi and I are...well, we're a lot smaller and people in nearby counties know when we're on the move."

Everyone at the table laughed, but Kirk's words against

her ear said the most, "They've learned to walk like ghosts to avoid becoming one, *anoshi*." Regi froze as the reality of his words sank in to her soul. She'd never really stopped to consider the enormity of what each man at the table had contributed to the world she lived in and how many times they'd put themselves in harm's way to protect the lives of others.

Regi's mother's words rang through her mind so clearly it was almost as if she were standing in the room. *'An attitude of gratitude, Regi…never forget the value of appreciating what other people do for you.'* She was surrounded by people who were willing to help her…because that is what they believed in, and she was humbled by that realization.

The least I can do is help them solve this puzzle, because right now neither they, nor their families are safe because of me. So get it together, Regina Sue, and figure this out.

Chapter Twelve

B RIAN WATCHED CARL Phillips turn the pendant around studying the symbols on the back. He'd typed a couple of searches on Mayan symbols into his phone's browser, but had struggled to read the small script until Regi had convinced him that she knew what the symbols meant. Brian had to hold back his grin at her indignant expression as she'd told Carl she could read the symbols, she just didn't know how they applied to the numbers written on the page. When the other men at the table had blinked at her in confusion, she'd explained. "Think of it this way. You have all worked crossword puzzles and riddles, right?" When they all nodded, she'd continued, "And those were written in English and I'll bet you all knew what each word meant, but that didn't mean you knew the answer to the puzzle." They'd all nodded their understanding and Brian had been impressed with her ability to explain it in a way that made sense.

He'd leaned over and spoken softly against her ear, "Just remember, baby, we aren't used to seeing you as an academic. Your business management skills are easy to recognize, but this antiquities expert persona is a new side of you. It might take a bit of time for us to all adjust." As he'd been speaking, he'd moved his hand up the inside of her thigh until the tips of his fingers were whispering soft touches against the outer lips of her sex. "Master Kirk and I have always seen the brilliant woman behind the mask, but even we may have underestimated you—so be patient as we all work on redefining our view." He'd deliberately started pitching his voice lower and was pleased to see her respond perfectly. Watching Regi's breathing hitch and seeing the pulse at the base of her neck speed up as he teased her swelling folds was pushing his own control to its limit. And he was about to suggest they leave the puzzle with Carl when he was saved the trouble.

"Regi, if you don't mind, I'd like to take this home with me. I think better in my own environment and I want to check on a couple of logic patterns because I'm fairly certain that is what was used along with the Mayan dual number system. I'm not sure exactly how to apply what I suspect has been done so I want to be able to focus on it. Hell, the only thing I'm sure of is that whoever did this was fucking brilliant." The man's face tinted the tiniest bit when he realized he'd said the last sentence out loud. Regi had assured him it wasn't a problem even though both he and Kirk had felt her body stiffen at the thought of being without the pendant she always wore.

As Carl made his way toward the back door, the others began drifting back to what they'd been doing before the impromptu meeting. Finally only Dean and Dell were left sitting with them. Dean looked considerately at Regi, "Sweetheart, we want you to know we've already made arrangements for a salvage boat complete with all the equipment necessary for diving and recovery. It will be waiting for us at a small marina in Belize City by tomorrow morning. When you get the coordinates, you just let us know and we'll put everything in motion." The three of them were all staring at the elder Wests completely stunned.

Dell laughed, "Damn, I love surprising people. It doesn't happen that often…hell, our Lilly usually knows what we're going to do before we do."

"That's because she plans everything and then convinces us it was our idea."

"True." Dell returned his attention to Regi, "But this was a pure pleasure, I promise you. But don't go thinking there isn't a catch, because there is. Lilly wants to go along, and you know that means Dean and I'll be along as well, because where she goes, we go."

This time Dell directed his words to Brian and Kirk, "When a woman captures your heart, you don't want her out of your sight for long. And when she is as fearless as our Lilly, you don't dare." After they'd all shared a laugh, Dell let the smile fade from his face as he stood, "We'll be waiting for your call. There isn't any question but what you'll have to figure out is what your parents found that has so many different folks all stirred up. I think it's about time the tail wagged the dog for a change, don't you?" Even as enigmatic as the comment was, Brian had to smile because it was also crystal clear.

Brian looked over at Regi after Dean and Dell had sauntered away to see her lost in thought. "I think they are telling you it's time to stop playing defense, baby."

"And I think they are right. I do believe I'd like to play this from the other direction for a while. I don't remember a lot about what we'd found in the wreck, I know Dad was still cataloging each piece's specific location. However, he was making an extraordinary effort to conceal its location. It was usual for us to anchor a short distance from a site, but this one was different for some reason. We were a long way from where we dove every day and that was really slowing our progress."

"Kirk and I are both certified for deep water diving and we'll be calling in a couple of colleagues to cover our practice while we're gone." When she started to protest, Brian put his finger over her lips, "We happen to agree with Dell. When your woman is fearless, you don't dare let her out of your sight for very long." He knew his smile had softened his declaration that she was *theirs* and he was enormously pleased she hadn't chosen to argue the point.

Kirk used his fingers to gently turn her face back to his, "Are you finished for the day, *anoshi*?" Since it wasn't a regular club day, most of the staff set their own hours and left whenever they'd completed whatever tasks had needed done. Brian suspected she'd hurried through whatever she'd needed to do so she could go upstairs and see the babies.

"Yes, I've been done for a while. I was upstairs helping Tobi. She was tired and cranky. But I think the bubble bath and alone time helped her feel more like herself. That little Kodi is a pistol. She is as bright eyed and spirited as her mama. And her daddies are going to have her spoiled rotten in no time at all." Brian could see the wistful look in her eyes and wondered if she wasn't thinking about what it would be like to cradle her own child in her arms. "But little Kameron is a joy. He looks up at you with those soulful eyes and you feel like he is wrapping himself around your heart."

Brian pulled her to her feet and held her hands firmly in his own leaving Kirk to smooth out her dress. "Come on, baby. You deserve some pampering, and I have just the answer."

THEY'D SETTLED REGI in her own bubble bath with candles surrounding her and soft music playing before they moved to their office and started making calls. It didn't take long for them to track down the two young physicians they had already been negotiating with in hopes of bringing them on board. Both were more than willing to make the switch and in less than an hour they'd all reached an agreement. He and Brian leaned back in their chairs and smiled at the progress they'd made. The two of them had worked hard to rebuild their practice after moving it from downtown Austin a couple of years ago. It had been lean for a while, but when word had started spreading about their attention to detail and their dedication to their patients' care, their numbers had grown rapidly.

"You know our staff is going to be thrilled, right?" Kirk laughed at Brian's question because the nurses working for them had almost become their second family, and they had all been encouraging them to bring on more staff for some time. "And we'll need a couple more nurses as well. Our team is already working non-stop, two more doctors will be entirely too much. Besides, they've been nagging us about taking time to smell the roses and I'll bet you dollars to donuts none of them have used any of their vacation time."

Kirk nodded, "Agreed." He called the agency they'd used and made sure their office manager and head nurse were given the final say when approving any new hires. They'd learned a long time ago that one of the secrets to a successful practice was making sure your staff was happy. Empowering them to decide who they worked with one small change that had made a huge difference.

Just as he finished his call, he heard a soft knock on the door. Looking up to see Regi standing in the doorway dressed in one of his dress shirts, her hair flowing in soft waves over her shoulders, stole his breath. He simply held out his hand to her when he felt her unease and smiled when she walked to him. "We were just getting ready to come to you. We've made all the arrangements to be free to travel with you. And I must say I'm looking forward to seeing you in a bikini."

"Oh yeah, and seeing you in a wetsuit is going to supply me with enough erotic dreams to keep the boat rocking all night long, baby." Kirk was grateful for Brian's ability to tease Regi just enough to drain some of the tension she was feeling from her small frame.

"Now, we'd planned to take you out on to a river boat for dinner, but I think the call we got from Carl a little while ago may change those plans." Kirk wasn't surprised to hear her gasp.

"He figured it out already? Holy shit, he is amazing."

Kirk couldn't have agreed more. In truth, the men at Prairie Winds never ceased to impress him. Their physical conditioning was second to none, but he'd often thought their intelligence was vastly under-acknowledged. He suspected that most of the former Special Forces members he'd met at Prairie Winds would test out in the genius range. "He has not only figured it out, he's also plotted it. And the others have already set things in motion for our travel if you're game. According to Jax, the location Carl has marked is approximately 2 miles from where you were found. So everything seems to be lining up."

The light dancing in her eyes was pure Regi-magic and he could practically hear her mind spinning as she took in everything he'd said. Brian stepped forward and pulled her into his arms, kissing the top of her head. "There is one small glitch though. The box had some sort of activation switch for a location device. The signal was caught quickly by Prairie Winds security and scrambled, but evidently it is old enough no one is sure if it was shut down fast enough."

"So my dad had booby-trapped the secret part of the box so he'd know if it was opened?" When Brian nodded, she continued, "That doesn't make any sense unless he assumed he'd be around if it fell out of his or mom's hands." Kirk could see the confusion in her eyes and the same questions the Prairie Winds team had been asking were quickly forming in her mind. What Charlie Hendricks had shared with everyone but Regi, was that he'd known her dad for a long time. He had actually help set up the ruse that saved her parents' lives but hadn't known Regi was going to be involved. No one had imagined at the time the couple would have to stay gone so long. But Kirk had to agree with the retired agent's assessment that hastily made plans rarely worked out as they were intended.

Regi pulled out of Brian's embrace and began pacing the length of the room. They'd seen her do the same thing at the club one day when she'd been trying to work through a problem in the bookkeeping. It was fascinating to listen to her as she practically narrated her thoughts. "You know, I Googled my grandmother's name last week and she died about a month ago. I was surprised I hadn't read about it in the news, but then I guess the leaders of crime families aren't big news like they used to be. I only remember meeting her a few times, although I'm sure it was more often than that.

"I don't remember that much about her, except she was beautiful and so very intense that even as a child I realized she was trying to intimidate me. My dad was terrified she was going to use me to force him into the family business and I'm sure he was probably right. He was wrong so rarely about anything, it doesn't seem likely he'd be off about his own mother. And even though I still don't know exactly what all *the family* business entails, I have a pretty good idea the illegal sale of antiquities was high on the list. So I'm guessing my dad found something of tremendous value, it's the only reason I can think of for all his efforts to conceal the location.

"I'm ready to leave whenever I can get a new passport. I'll have to buy clothes once we arrive in Belize since mine are still being scanned at Prairie Winds. I can hardly wait to dive again. It's been a long time since I've been down, damn I'm probably going to have to test out again. I hate tests." She was definitely on a roll and Kirk really hated for her to waste energy stalking the length of the room when it could be put to much more satisfying use.

This time when she paced by him, Kirk shackled her wrist and spun her into his arms. "Travel arrangements are being handled, including an updated passport for you. Lilly has nominated herself as your official shopper. She and Tobi are ravaging web sites with next day delivery as we speak. The Prairie Winds team is—in Kyle's words, going to be ready to go *wheels up in forty-eight*. So we've got some time to enjoy ourselves. I think it is time to quiet that busy mind of yours, *mi amõre*." Kirk felt her body go on alert even as she molded herself against his much larger frame. He'd been leaning against his desk and pulling her into the V of his legs meant his arousal was pressed against her thinly covered mound and he could already feel her heat through the layers of fabric. His desire for her would have been impossible to miss and when he saw the first flush move over her chest and up her neck, he wanted to lean down and follow it all the way up with his tongue.

"There are so very many options, I'm not sure where

to begin. But I know we need to feed you first because once we start I'm sure we won't be visiting the kitchen again for quite a while." He kissed the tip of her nose and turned her into Brian's waiting arms. "See if you can wind up our little doll a bit while I re-heat our dinner." They'd already ordered take-out and left it in the kitchen while she'd finished her bath. The phone calls they'd taken and the dark circles under her beautiful eyes when they'd settled her in the steaming tub had changed their plans.

While he worked in the kitchen, Kirk could hear Brian speaking softly to Regi and her soft moans of arousal. His partner was going to have their sweet subbie in quite a state by the time dinner was ready. While he waited for the microwave to finish, Kirk considered how his trained Dominant side had always recognized it was his number one responsibility to care for any submissive who put herself in his care. And he had always placed that duty to be above all others during their scenes together. But everything was different with Regi. Caring for her wasn't a duty—it was an honor and privilege. That realization brought him up short. *She's the one.* His *shiichoo* had always told him the Great Spirit would whisper his blessing when the time was right, but Kirk hadn't expected it to be so clear, nor had he expected it to be accompanied by the ding of a microwave oven. Grinning to himself, he set the dishes on the table and called his future in to the room.

Chapter Thirteen

CHARLIE LEANED BACK in his favorite recliner making no attempt to hold back his exhausted sigh. Even the smallest physical exertion was draining. Dying slowly was excruciating and his respect for patients whose battles with chronic diseases lasted for years continued to rocket upward. The work he'd finalized today had taken everything he had, but his inner clock had been ticking so loudly the past few days it had been impossible to ignore. All of the final details were signed, sealed, and delivered. Even his last letter to Regina was in his attorney's hands. Tipping back a bottle of his favorite imported beer, he stared without seeing as his alma mater trounced their biggest rival. Ordinarily he'd have been cheering loudly but the overwhelming fatigue was keeping him from enjoying their sweet victory.

When the commentators began rehashing every moment of the game he moved to the bar and retrieved another beer. *There is nothing as annoying as having some ass wipe tell me what I just saw. Thanks for the insight, piss ant, I'd have never figured out why they won by twenty-one points without you telling me.* Settling back in his chair, Charlie felt his presence before he was actually able to make out Mark Stephano's silhouette in the shadows.

"What took you so long? I've been wondering how long it would take you to show up." Holding up his half-empty bottle he added, "The rest of the beer isn't going to drink itself you know." Charlie inclined his head toward the bar and watched as the man he'd once considered a friend move quietly behind the carved wood bar toward the large glass fronted refrigerator against the back wall. Even now, a decade later, Mark Stephano moved with the grace of the predator he'd always been—silent and deadly. The larger shadow that Charlie was sure accompanied Mark everywhere he went didn't move and Charlie chose to ignore the implications.

Mark slouched onto the leather sofa. When Charlie simply raised a brow at his uninvited, but not unexpected guest's sigh, it sounded as if the weight of what lay ahead was just beginning to settle over him. When Mark finally looked up at Charlie the sadness in his eyes was easy to see. "At first I didn't have a way to return—or maybe I just didn't see it as an option worth pursuing. Anyway, after I lost my beloved Nalia, I didn't care about anything for a long time. She represented everything I always wanted to be. She had a purity to her spirit, an honesty tested by the fire of her personality that made me a better person just by her presence. That light of goodness faded from me just as quickly as Nalia was stolen from my arms, and my fall into the abyss was fast and ugly."

Charlie knew his expression must have betrayed his skepticism because Mark shrugged adding, "I'm not saying this excuses what I've done, but I hope it explains it—at least in part." His pause and regretful expression spoke almost as loud as his words.

"For what it's worth, I was sorry to hear about Nalia—I always liked her. I've seen her spirit shining in Regina's eyes more times than I can count. Your daughter shares a lot of your same interests, hell, she even looks a little like you, but the fire that burns in her heart is pure Nalia."

Mark's smile was genuine and Charlie wondered how rarely it happened. "I wish…more than you know…that things could be different. I've made so many mistakes, but things are beyond my control now." Once again Charlie was surprised by the regret he heard in Mark's voice, and even though he had a lot of regrets in his own life, he would leave this world knowing he'd done everything he could to square things with Regi. Without a doubt, there were things he should have told her, but she'd already been drowning in grief and fear, adding to that burden hadn't been in her best interest in the beginning. Then, as time had gone on, she'd blossomed and they'd become each other's family. In truth, she had added so much joy to his life his decision to keep quiet had quickly become an entirely selfish one, because he'd feared losing her forever if she knew the truth about how he'd come to be the first person on the boat that day.

"How did you find her after all this time?" Charlie wasn't stalling for time, he knew there was no point. He was simply curious and knew Mark well enough that he was sure the man wouldn't hesitate to brag…and his guest didn't take long to prove him right. There wasn't any doubt Mark had found Regina or he wouldn't be here. This trip was all about tying up loose ends.

"The box had two triggers. It was brilliantly made if I do say so myself. The first switch was designed to send out a locator signal for just a few seconds because I was certain that once someone recognized what they were holding they would shield the main trigger. I really expected another agency man to find it long before now. My hope had been to find it before it was opened. And to be honest I don't know exactly where it is, but I do know someone set off the first trigger and then the second one blinked on the screen just a few times before disappearing behind a wash of static—probably some kind of scrambler. I know the approximate physical location of both signals, but I'm betting it's not anywhere near Austin or the Prairie Winds Club now."

"Why would you think that?"

"Because Kent and Kyle West's parents' private jet left Austin about an hour ago. Their flight plan hasn't appeared anywhere yet and that tells me the kink brothers may not be as *retired* as they claim to be." Charlie could hear the underlying steel in Mark's voice, he was nearing the edge of his patience.

"What could possibly be in that box that you need so badly?"

Charlie hadn't expected an answer to his question and was genuinely surprised when Mark responded, "Coordinates. It was one of the few times I didn't make a duplicate set. I thought if Regina got them off the boat, I'd be able to retrieve them from her within the first year, but when that didn't work out…" Charlie didn't ask about what Mark had left unsaid, mostly because he was just too tired to listen any longer. The emotional exhaustion of writing the letter to Regi and the physical strain of the trip to finish the last of the details at his lawyer's small office were pushing him closer and closer to sleep.

Feeling the press of his Sig Suer, which was tucked between his thigh and the side of the recliner gave him a sudden sense of freedom. The sharp tone of Mark's voice brought him back to the moment, "Where are they headed?"

"No clue. And even if I did know I wouldn't tell you." Charlie studied the man he'd once trusted and wondered if his wife's untimely death had really been the catalyst for his fall or if the darkness had started much earlier than anyone knew. Nalia Stephano had been a brilliant mathematician, much more so than her husband had ever given her credit for. They'd met when she had been doing work for a European think tank and she'd thrown away a promising career to follow the charming young man she thought was a treasure hunter. Charlie didn't remember all the details of their union, but he did know if Regi was right about the note containing coded numbers in her mother's writing, then it was likely Nalia had discovered her husband's duplicity and had begun taking a more proactive stance in protecting her own interests. The fact she'd been shot by someone gunning for Mark had been a senseless tragedy.

"What was on the last wreck that has been worth waiting a decade to retrieve?" Charlie would never understand why Mark hadn't reached out to Regi, but a small part of him would always be grateful the man had stepped away. Everything had changed for Charlie when Regi entered his life—she'd been a beacon of light, and she'd taught him what it was like to love and be loved unconditionally. She'd changed the way he lived his life because she had shown him there was a difference between surviving and living. He hoped the letter he'd written would convince her that she'd done far more for him than he'd ever done for her.

Mark sighed and Charlie saw his eyes flick to the unmoving shadow still lurking in the background. "Gold. Millions of dollars in gold and even more in priceless Mayan artifacts." Mark's long pause was Charlie's cue the discussion was over and in truth he was relieved. "This isn't the way I wanted this to end, you know."

Charlie couldn't hold back his chuckle at the absurdity of the situation, but winced at the pain it caused. It was time...he knew it and was at peace with his decision. "I know. Let me see if I can't help you." With those words he moved to wrap his hand around the grip of his Sig and pulled the weapon out of its hiding place. Even though it was loaded, he had not chambered a round because he hadn't wanted to accidently shoot Mark in hopes that someday he and Regi would be able to rebuild their relationship. As expected, the movement from the shadows was swift and decisive. The flash of the weapon was the last thing Charlie saw.

Chapter Fourteen

REGI FIDGETED IN her seat as the SUV she was riding in parked near the end of the wood-planked dock a short distance from the main marina. She could already smell the salty air tinged with the pungent aroma of fish and knew the first wave of local trawlers would have already returned to unload their early morning catch. She had always loved the energy that surrounded marinas, because it was deceptively nonchalant. While the fishermen appeared to be easy going, there was always an undercurrent of urgency because their livelihoods were so dependent upon the whims of Mother Nature. After settling in west Texas, Regi had soon discovered the farmers and ranchers of that region faced the same challenges. She'd often marveled at the fact that despite all civilizations advances, people still depended on the good graces of God to provide them with food.

True to his word, Kyle had gotten them in the air in less than forty-eight hours after Carl had solved her mother's coded message. They'd spent the better part of another forty-eight hours traveling and getting a good night's sleep before they'd filled several vehicles to make the short trip to the pier. Regi was still shaking her head at how easily money could expedite *anything and everything*. Even though her parents had been fairly wealthy, she'd been so young when she lost them, she hadn't understood all the ways their money and connections had helped her. Then she'd spent so much of the past decade struggling to make ends meet so her appreciation for money was very real. After she'd taken the job at Prairie Winds, she'd stashed every spare bit of cash she could scrape together, knowing she would inevitably have to move and start over yet again.

Regi had to admit that working for the Wests had given her a sense of security she hadn't even realized she attained until recently. She might have taken that sense of safety for granted, but she had never stopped appreciating the close-knit group of friends that surrounded her. Brian's soft kiss against her temple brought her out of her thoughts. She looked around realizing they were the only ones still sitting in the vehicle.

"A penny for your thoughts, baby. You seemed so absorbed in whatever was on your mind I wanted to give you a couple of extra moments to work it out. But the others are loaded and waiting, so we need to get going." Brian's voice was soft with understanding and she appreciated that he wasn't annoyed with her for holding up the rest of the crew.

Snuggling against his warmth was too much temptation and for a few moments Regi just let herself absorb his strength while she tried to wrap her mind around what they were about to do. Once she'd managed to find an even keel again, she pulled back and smiled, "Thank you. I needed a minute to pull everything back together. There are just so many unanswered questions. So many bits and pieces of my memory that are suddenly beginning to surface, I can hardly process it all. And hearing the news this morning about Charlie broke my heart. He was always there for me even though we met under very questionable circumstances, I do think he ended up caring about me on some level."

Finding out her friend and mentor was gone had shaken her, but she was grateful his suffering had been cut short. When Kyle called, he hadn't given her any details, but she'd been too stunned to think clearly enough to ask him much either. She'd known Charlie's condition had started to deteriorate quickly when the cancer stopped responding to treatment, but the end had come much quicker than she had anticipated. And even though hearing Charlie had passed wasn't completely unexpected, it certainly added significantly to her emotional upheaval. She needed to call Kyle again this evening and ask for more information because, in truth, she hadn't heard much past his initial words. She'd heard Charlie was gone and hadn't hesitated to pass the phone to Kirk and lose herself in the shelter of Brian's arms.

As they walked toward the boat, Regi felt her energy and hope returning. There was something about the ocean, which always seemed to reset the deepest part of her in a way nothing else had ever been able to. Being so far away from the Gulf of Mexico had been her only objection to moving to Austin.

If they were right about the location, then the topography maps showed the wreck was likely resting right along an underwater ridge. The wreck itself probably wasn't very deep, but the area was riff with superstitions that had kept the locals from making any attempts to search for the ship rumored to have been carrying a Mayan queen's magical necklace. The water was fairly shallow by traditional salvaging standards and was the only reason it was accessible for a diver using traditional scuba gear.

The average depth of the western Caribbean Sea that

far from the shoreline would ordinarily be too deep to explore without more specialized equipment. Regi remembered her father's concern about the stability of the wreck, but he'd never let her dive near the starboard side of the sunken ship so she didn't know exactly what to expect today. The only thing she knew for sure was whatever was down there had likely cost her parents their lives. And if she wanted to be free of her fear of *the family* she had to unravel all the circumstances surrounding that day. She'd originally been told her mom and dad had fallen victim to local gang members who'd gotten wind of the American's find. But when nothing had added up, Charlie had finally admitted her dad's refusal to return to *the family* had led to their deaths. Now once again things weren't lining up and she had to wonder if she'd ever know the truth about the afternoon that changed the course of her entire life.

Stepping on to the deck of the boat the Wests had rented was like coming home again and Regi felt as if everything inside her had suddenly calmed. Kirk had been standing a few feet from her, but looked up immediately and the smile that spread over his face warmed her heart. His long strides brought him to her side in seconds and his eyes had never left hers. "Tell me," was all he said but she instinctively knew exactly what he meant.

"I don't know if I can explain it. Just feeling the gentle motion of the boat beneath my feet re-set something in me. I was suddenly overwhelmed with confidence I'm finally on the right path. As thrilled as I am with the feeling, it confuses me too." She laughed because she knew her words didn't make sense, but it didn't change the fact they were true.

Kirk's half smile reassured her that he had indeed understood what she'd meant. "I can feel the change in you and it's remarkable. Thank you for sharing it with me." Looking into his eyes, Regi knew his words had been sincere and for a self-proclaimed land lover she assumed that was a fairly significant concession. Kirk had insisted he didn't mind sailing…that he simply preferred to spend time riding his horse over his family's beloved west Texas ranch. But Brian had told her that even though Kirk was an excellent swimmer and certified diver, he rarely ventured onto larger boats because he dreaded losing sight of land. "Your spirit soars here and I'm anxious to see it soar when you look out over the valleys on the ranch one day soon." He smiled at her and then waved his hand toward the dive deck, "Go check your equipment, *anoshi*, we're ready to cast-off and according to the calculations, we'll be at the site by the time you are ready."

It hadn't taken long at all to make the trip to their dive site, but Regi spent the time making sure everything was ready and reviewing with the diving pro onboard so she was prepared for what was to come. Lilly had joined her, and Regi found she enjoyed answering all of Lilly's questions because it had been a wonderful distraction as well as a chance for Regi to get her mind focused on diving again after being away from it for so long. Regi could already see Lilly was going to maneuver her way into becoming certified and she had to hold back her grin when the dive master flashed Regi a knowing grin.

"Damn those husbands of mine for not letting me take the scuba lessons I signed up for last fall. They swore I'd just end up pissing off Neptune. Hell, I thought they were talking about the planet until I found out that was just another name for Poseidon. And why on earth would the Greek God of the Sea not like me? Pish-posh…it was just an excuse if you ask me. And look now…I'm missing out on a perfectly good adventure because of their overprotectiveness."

Dell West stepped up behind his wife and wrapped his arms protectively around her as he leaned over her shoulder to watch Regi. "We aren't overprotective, my love, we are simply experienced in your wily ways. And watching you disappear into the deep blue waters of the Caribbean Sea without one of us alongside you would scare the hell out of me." With a quick wink at Regi, he added, "And consider those two lovely grandchildren of ours. They need their sweet granny, after all no one else would ever be able to spoil them as good as you will. Who will advocate for them when their daddies' try to pretend they weren't the terrors of west Texas? Remember, our lovely daughter-in-law doesn't have a mama either and she'd be heartbroken if she lost you."

Regi had to give the man credit, he was pulling out all the stops, and from the softening expression on Lilly's face his efforts were not in vain. After Lilly had turned in his arms, Regi gave him a quick thumbs up and went back to work. At this point everything she did was simply busy work, but she needed to keep her hands and mind busy to prevent the sudden waves of unease that were moving over her.

MARK STOOD IN the shadows of the wheelhouse and watched his daughter walk down the pier with one of the doctors he knew were currently sheltering her. Once he'd gotten the first ping on the box's location it hadn't taken his men long to learn everything about Regina and the people who surrounded her. He also knew the Wests' sudden interest in renting diving and salvage equipment had stirred up other interested parties as well, and that had meant he was going to have to move more quickly than he'd planned. Ideally, he'd have let them find the wreck and then move in to retrieve the lion's share out from under their noses, but that was no longer an option. For the first time Mark wondered if the agency hadn't been watching Regi as well. If so, perhaps the man who had sold him out years ago hadn't been working alone. Whoever had searched Regi's apartment had been good, but obviously his daughter had inherited her mother's intelligence because the thugs hadn't found the box.

There was a lot of scuttlebutt and innuendo floating around about the West brothers' involvement in a newly formed group of contract do-gooders. They were going to be an inconvenience to his business if the rumors turned out to be true. And while it seemed unlikely they could have already made enough enemies their employees would be targeted, anything was possible.

The meeting with Charlie had shaken him more than he'd expected it to. Mark had known the instant his former friend made the decision to end their discussion, what he hadn't fully understood until later was why. Mark had seen something dark move through Charlie's eyes several times during their conversation and his exhaustion had been almost palpable.

Discovering Charlie's weapon hadn't even been ready to fire had stolen Mark's breath. He'd been baffled by the former agent's actions until he'd learned that his friend had been dealing with crushing pain and was living on a very short amount of borrowed time. Charlie hadn't been at all surprised to see him, and the copies of the legal work setting on his former friend's desk confirmed he'd likely been tipped off that Mark was coming.

Even though Mark would have sworn he'd lost his final thread of humanity the moment Nalia stopped breathing, seeing the vacant look in his former friend's eyes after his bodyguard ended the man's life with a single shot had brought on an unwelcome flood of emotion. The night he'd held his beloved Nalia in his arms as the life drained out of her had flashed in his mind, like a never-ending reel from a horror movie he couldn't escape. Even now, the memory of that night nearly made his knees buckle as he stood by watching his only child make her way to the waiting boat. While he knew there was no going back, watching as Regina walked by...so near, yet so far...sparked something in him that he had thought long dead.

The small crew he'd brought along was ready and waiting to cast off at his order, but Mark wasn't in a hurry. They'd placed locators on the boat the Wests had rented so they had the luxury of following at a safe distance and letting the former SEALs aboard lead them right to the site. Mark had been surprised to learn Kent and Kyle West sent some of their *employees* along and even more surprised to learn their parents were on board as well. They'd either grossly underestimated the danger or they were enormously arrogant about the abilities of the few men accompanying their family and friend. Only time would tell which was true.

SAGE MCCALL LEANED against the wall watching the man identified as Mark Stephano. Kyle had caught up with the three of them just before they'd boarded the last flight on their way home. He and his brother, Sam, had reluctantly put their new bride on the flight to Austin and then boarded another flight bringing them to Belize. Jen hadn't been thrilled about being left out of the mission, but three new babies at home had persuaded her to sit this one out.

He and Sam had been on the ground before the Wests' jet had landed and watched in amusement as the amateurs Stephano employed put locators on the boat Dean and Dell had chartered. It hadn't taken any time at all to tap into the units' signal and patch it through to Micah Drake back at Prairie Winds. Sage smiled to himself thinking about how much fun Micah was going to have re-routing the asshats that were responsible for Charlie Hendricks' death.

Kyle had told them Regi didn't know all the details, and Sage wondered how she'd take the news once this was resolved. Sage had only known Regi for a short time but he liked her, and the more he learned about her background the more he admired her as well. He heard his brother walk up and smiled at Sam's softly muttered curses. "The bugs on his boat are working and I want to blow the bastards up just because they are too arrogant to live. I swear if any of them grow up to reproduce we'll get negative karma points so we really should just blow the boat now."

Sage finally lost the battle to hold back his laughter, "Jesus, you are an ass. We haven't been away from Jen for two full days and you're already turning into a homicidal maniac. Fuck, it scares me to death to think what you might have done if we'd been deployed after we married her. You probably would have become some sort of weapon of mass destruction. Hell, mom would have been pissed seven ways to Sunday if your name became synonymous with insanity—death and destruction wouldn't have been a problem, but insanity would have annoyed the shit out of her."

Sam laughed as Sage had hoped he would, "Yeah, yeah, what-the-fuck-ever. Where do you think I got my *crazy-gene*? Sure as hell didn't come from Dad."

Sage snorted a laugh and agreed. Hell, their dad was one of the most levelheaded people he knew. He and Sam had wondered more than once how their wild-card mother and even keeled father had ever managed to hook up. "True enough, seems I'm the calm one lately and my only regret is that I don't have any witnesses."

"Har-fucking-har. I just came to tell you that we've found out where Stephano and his merry band of master-bates have been staying. Let's go see what we can find out. Hopefully they've left out an outline of their criminal history and plans to save us some time."

"Hmmm, they have medication for delusions, you know." Sage hadn't been able to hide the amusement from his voice and his brother's grin told him it hadn't been missed. They took off toward the small car they'd rented. Folding their tall frames into what was essentially a glorified enclosed golf cart, he shook his head. "Christ Almighty, this car reminds me of that death-trap of Jen's."

"You wanna talk about delusions? You thinking our sweet woman isn't going to find out what you've done on that front is pretty fucking delusional too, asshole." Sam's words were hollow because he was involved up to his eyeballs in the plan to get rid of Jen's Mini Cooper, but at least he wasn't stupid enough to think they'd get away with it.

BREAKING IN TO the small bungalow Stephano was renting along the beach had been child's play. *God, I love arrogant douchebags, they make life so much easier for those of us who have actually trained for our jobs.* Sam couldn't remember the last time they'd had an easier time getting past a security system and he wondered for a minute if it hadn't been some sort of set-up, but their double check confirmed the system was indeed just that—cheap. *Un-fucking-believable. The man is reported to be worth nearly a billion dollars but relies on a system a third grader with a screwdriver and a ball of twine could get around.*

It didn't take Sam long to find the file folders Stephano had on Regi, Charlie, and the Wests. Holding them up for Sage to see, Sam observed, "You can't fault the man's information team, it looks like they've done a pretty decent job of gathering Intel in a relatively short span of time. Too bad his security guys aren't as diligent." Sam used the hand-held scanner from their small bag of tricks to copy each page, forwarding them to the Prairie Winds control room as he did. "Let's get out of here, I don't see anything that tells us what our team is walking into and quite frankly I'm not that interested in reading Kent and Kyle's bios." *Hell, I've known them long enough to write the damn things. What I don't know is why they don't just let me blow the asshat up and call it a day.*

Chapter Fifteen

I T DIDN'T TAKE Regi long to see the reason her parents had worked so hard to conceal the location of the small shipwreck. Her dad had only let her see a small portion of the cargo when she'd joined him that last day, and now she understood why. She'd known he had only allowed her to tag along because she'd nagged him mercilessly. But now, as an adult, she had a much better understanding of why he'd tried to conceal the magnitude of the find.

Regi had spotted the markers right away and used a handheld blower to move the sediment until she found the edge of the mesh covering her dad had used to shield the cargo from surface detectors. She hadn't missed the quick hand signals the SEALs had flashed at one another. There was no doubt Dex Raines and Ash Moore had quickly noted the enormous monetary value teetering so precariously on the unstable ledge. The divers would need to use caution and avoid all quick or exaggerated movements that might cause rapid shifts in the water near the salvage site. It looked like it would be a slow and arduous recovery.

Brian opted to go down with her first after everyone had agreed leaving one of the physician's on board at all times was in the entire crew's best interest. He hadn't left her side and when he thought she was too close to the boat's unstable starboard side he'd let her know quickly that her safety trumped all concerns about recovering the gold that had been lost to the sea so many years ago. Regi moved toward the stern and brushed aside a thick layer of sediment, and froze. She couldn't believe what she was seeing. The small statues were positioned in a perfect circle and Regi knew they'd once been nestled safely in an ornately carved box befitting their sacred nature.

There were mentions of the lost statues in various texts, but no one had ever been able to verify their existence, because the truth had vanished with the Mayan people after the golden statues were lost to thieves. For several seconds she couldn't move and hadn't ever realized she was holding her breath until Brian grabbed her arm and shook her. She frantically pointed to the circle of statues and then placed her hand over her heart so he'd sense their importance. After she'd taken several pictures of their precise layout, she slipped them in her shoulder sling. The fact there were thirteen statues would have been confirmation of their Mayan origin even if she hadn't recognized the deities represented. Thirteen was an important number in the Mayan culture and seeing the answer to so many questions laying in perfect form right in front of her brought tears to Regi's eyes.

The dive team quickly photo-documented the entire site and recovered enough to make a case for financing a larger recovery effort before making their way slowly back to the surface. By the time they climbed back aboard the boat Regi was nearly hyperventilating from excitement. She leapt into Kirk's arms and wrapped her legs around his waist as she squealed, "Oh my God in heaven, you simply won't believe what we found. The golden statues...the ones no one has ever even been able to prove existed...they were right there and I got all the pics of their placement before I bagged them. If I never find another artifact in my life I'll be forever grateful for this moment." She gave him a kiss and then slid down his large frame and turned to the Wests who were all standing to the side smiling at her indulgently. She hugged each one of them and then laughed through her tears of joy as she apologized for getting them wet.

After they'd cleaned and stored their equipment, they carefully unloaded all the heavy crates carrying a variety of "finds" they'd hoisted to the surface. Regi was just finishing up when she felt the boat begin moving back to shore. From this point forward the wreck would be salvaged by a professional team. Dean and Dell West had already begun making calls and promised her that she'd have first rights to artifacts and the salvage company they'd talked to had agreed to take their share out of the gold. It wasn't a large concession on their part since gold bars would be much easier to convert to cash than artifacts that any one of several Central American nations might easily attempt to claim.

Regi didn't think Kirk had appeared terribly disappointed he wouldn't be diving to the wreck site, but when he tugged her down the narrow passageway to the shower she started wondering if she was going to be his "consolation prize." He closed the door and then turned to her, "You think I am in need of consoling, *anoshi*? I got to see the woman who has claimed my heart bob to the surface, surrounded by glittering diamonds of sunlight dancing atop crystal blue water with a look of pure joy on her face today. Then she leapt into my arms as she wrapped her beautiful legs around my waist pressing her warmth against my cock and her breasts to my chest. Joy and excitement bubbled from her in a tumble of words telling me about the treasure she'd found and it all ended with her sweet lips pressed against mine. So tell me, what in all that would cause me grief?"

His hands had been slowly removing the cover-up she'd pulled on over her swimsuit. Kirk's eyes never left hers as he untied the strings of the tiniest bikini she'd ever seen and let the aquamarine colored pieces drop to the floor. When she'd seen the suit Lilly had purchased, Regi hadn't been surprised. The look on both Kirk's and Brian's faces had made her laugh because their expressions had reminded her of the cartoon characters whose eyes bulged out of their sockets.

Regi reached forward and grabbed the hem of Kirk's shirt before the trained submissive in her woke up and took notice. She froze in place waiting for his nod of approval before pulling it over his head. Slipping her fingers into his waistband, she once again paused until he'd nodded his head ever so slightly before she unfastened the cargo shorts he wore. When she pushed the shorts down his narrow hips she was thrilled to see he'd gone commando because his cock sprang up to great her. He was already hard and the heat pulsing from his rigid length moved against her sensitive skin as she pressed against him. "I can't wait to slide inside of your tight pussy, but make no mistake, *mi amõre*, seeing the joy in your eyes was worth every second I agonized about your safety while you were diving. And *this*?" he asked as he slid deep inside her, "Oh I assure you this is what inspires poets and songwriters to bless the world with words and melodies that hold us enthralled."

Hearing Kirk's words spoken with such passion plunged Regi into the depths of a blinding orgasm before she'd even realized she was close. *Why did I fight them for so long? At times my ability to sabotage what is in my best interest knows no bounds.*

Kɪʀᴋ ꜰᴇʟᴛ ʟɪᴋᴇ his body was going to erupt into flames. His cock was so engorged and sensitive by the time he pushed into Regi, every flutter of her vaginal muscles tested the very limits of his control. And when he'd whispered against her ear the strength of her orgasm nearly overwhelmed him. As a submissive, she knew how and when to control her release, but he knew full well this one had blindsided her just as it had him. He'd captured her scream with a kiss as much to distract himself as to keep from confirming their actions to everyone onboard. Just as she started to come down from the first mountaintop he wrapped her wrists in his own and pulled her arms over her head. Regi had always responded beautifully to bondage and he watched her eyes flare with desire as she tugged against his hold.

"You'll stay exactly where I've put you. I plan to feel your release again, but this time you'll wait for permission like a good sub." Hearing her small gasp told him she hadn't realized until that moment that she'd stolen a release. "Aha, I see you know what you've done. We'll deal with that control problem, I promise you. I think Master Brian needs to see how long you can hold out against his light and magic show." Kirk was certain his friend had been holding back from using his favorite toy on Regi because he worried she would be frightened by the stories circulating the club circuit about a sub being severely burned a couple of years ago.

While the story was basically true, the most important factor in that accident had been the lack of training on the part of the Dom using the ultraviolet wand. The idiot had also used wax play earlier in the scene but hadn't extinguished all of the candles while his novice sub lay on a highly flammable covering he'd used on the table. Since the man hadn't wanted to be bothered with cleaning the equipment properly after using a petroleum based gel to remove wax from the sub's breasts he'd used a paper covering for the table so he could simply throw it away after their scene.

One of the club's dungeon monitors had stepped in just as the Dom made the first pass with the wand, but he'd been too late. The flash fire had burned the submissive so badly she would likely be suffering through painful skin grafts for the next several years. The club had blurred the faces of the principals and then shared the video with other clubs in their network so it could be used during training sessions for both Dominants and submissives. In all the time Kirk had been in medical school, he wasn't sure he'd ever seen or heard anything as chilling as that video.

Kirk was enormously pleased with Regi's response to his comment about Brian's ultraviolet wands even though he personally preferred floggers. Watching as her nipples tightened even further and seeing the flush of desire deepen until it looked like a beautiful rose sent another wave of heat to his already scorching cock. Brian never used the wands anywhere but in very specific areas and always had another Dom spotting him, and now Kirk was very grateful he'd been trained to use the device so he could act as his friend's backup.

Setting a random pace of deep and shallow thrusts intended to keep Regi from finding the predictable rhythm he knew she usually needed to reach orgasm, he could literally feel her pleasure as it pulsed around him. Her body was trying to keep him as deep inside her as the muscles could and he was quickly losing his own battle to stave off the plunge into the sweet oblivion of release. Regi was soon panting as she paid homage to gods that Kirk had never even heard of and when he felt lightning arc from his balls up his spine, he gave her the command she'd been waiting for, "Come for me, *anoshi*." Pushing in so deep he felt the jets of his release splash back on to the tip of his penis as he bathed her cervix with cum.

The ferocity of his release left him quaking with his cheek pressed against hers and his forehead pressed against the cool tile of the shower. He felt the quiver of over-exertion ripple through his thigh muscles and hoped like hell that he could keep his knees locked long enough to recover his strength so he didn't take them both down in the boat's tiny shower enclosure. *How does she do it? How does she manage to make each time more special than the one before? She owns me...heart and soul...it's all hers.*

THE GENTLE FORWARD movement of the boat was soothing and looking over the pieces they'd brought back to the surface humbled her. Lilly and her husbands stood nearby as Regi explained the pieces represented some of the rare examples of Mayan gold. "Despite the fact the Spaniards had expected to find vast amounts of gold when they came upon the Mayan people, the truth was what little gold these indigenous people had was usually gained in trade with the neighboring tribes. They understood how precious it was and used it to create figurines honoring their many gods, like the ones you see laying in the salt-water bath. We'll leave everything we bring up in salt water until a conservation specialist can take care of them. I'm not well versed in the newest methods and it's better for us to error on the side of caution by leaving the items out of any direct light and keeping them in the same water they have been in for so many years. The gold coins that were on board the ship were probably originally stolen from the Incas or Aztecs of other regions in Central America because those were the people with the large stores of the valuable metal European explorers had sailed across the Atlantic in search of." Regi paused for a few seconds and then laughed when she saw the puzzled looks on the men's faces. "I know what you're thinking and you are right. Those gold bars indicate the ship wasn't ancient despite the fact it carried so many incredibly old pieces."

"Regi, are you interested in working with the salvage team? We can stay for a few days if you'd like." Dell West's question surprised her. He was the quieter of Lilly's husbands, often letting his brother take the lead when Regi had seen them in social situations. Lilly had assured her that was an illusion, but his direct question still seemed out of character. According to his wife, Dell was perfectly content to let his brother be the face and voice of their businesses, but more often than not, he was the brilliance behind their decisions.

"Yes, I'd like that very much. I won't need to be here long. The ship wasn't a large one and surprisingly it is fairly intact. And anything that has fallen over the deep ledge belongs to Mother Nature now. I know there are robotics that could make attempts to explore the depths of that trench, but after seeing the outline of the ship I don't see any reason to even consider that." Because the Caribbean Sea wasn't as deep as either the Atlantic or Pacific Ocean people rarely considered the fact the fissures along its floor could still plunge to unimaginable depths because the fact was any crack in the Earth's mantle could be incredibly deep. Just the thought of being tangled in debris when it plummeted over the edge and into the trench's murky depths sent a shiver up her spine.

MARK STEPHANO WAS furious. They'd spent the entire day chasing their tails. By early afternoon he'd known they weren't anywhere near the wreck, hell, even considering Nalia's penchant for obscure mathematical codes and his inability to decipher them, it was clear they'd been led in the wrong direction. He'd continued for longer than he should despite the fact they hadn't once seen the small ship they were supposed to be tailing simply because he wanted to know who was tapped into their system. Mark had hoped to back-trace the signals to the source, but the phone call he'd gotten from his security office telling him the signals from the transponders were being rerouted and then bounced all over the place, making it impossible to track. He'd been so angry he'd nearly slung the sat-phone into the sea.

Since his people had been "eyes on" Regi and her eclectic entourage since they'd landed, Mark knew there had to have been boots already on the ground before the Wests' jet arrived. What he didn't know was who, how many, or what else they might know. He'd already been forced to step up his schedule once and he didn't relish the idea of doing it again. Because when you did that—mistakes were made, and his realization that he didn't have any other real option than to kick it up another notch wasn't setting well at all.

Mark had always hoped to reestablish at least some

semblance of a father-daughter relationship with Regina, but he knew her well enough to know if any of her friends were hurt as a result of his duplicity or actions, that would never happen. It was already going to be difficult to explain Charlie's death even though he hadn't been the one to pull the trigger.

Leaning against the bow's railing watching the blue water slide by, Mark felt as if every mistake he'd ever made was weighing heavily on his shoulders. His decision years ago to play both ends against the middle had been monumentally disastrous. And failing to level with Nalia hadn't been any better. The only *truth* in his adult life was that he'd loved his wife with everything he'd had. She had owned him from the moment she'd looked up from her work as he'd entered her small office. He had never believed in love at first sight, hell, considering the family he'd been raised in it was a miracle he'd even recognized the emotion when it slammed in to him with enough force to steal his breath.

She hadn't fallen for him nearly as easily, and for the first time in Mark's life he'd had to *win* the girl. His fellow agents had teased him mercilessly, but he had been determined. It had taken him several attempts to convince her to join him for dinner, when she'd finally reluctantly conceded, he'd made the evening impossible for her to forget. "She wouldn't want you to live in the past you know." Joey's voice startled Mark back to the moment. The eldest member of Mark's crew always seemed to know when he was struggling—and the elderly man would just appear at Mark's side. Mark had always considered Joey his safe haven in any emotional storm and had learned over the years to listen to his words of wisdom.

"You are right...as usual. I knew this would happen

when I returned to this place. She loved it here you know. And if I hadn't had to run, I think we would have eventually settled here." He'd evened the score with the man who had sold him out to the agency, but that hadn't changed anything. Mark had still been forced to seek his family's help and Nalia paid the ultimate price. She'd never taken his warnings about safety seriously because he had never bothered to tell her the truth. He would never forget the sick feeling of dread he'd had when he realized Nalia had stepped out on to the balcony of their suite. Mark had been a split second too late, the crack of the rifle had echoed in his dreams for years. She'd crumbled in to his arms and the light in her eyes had faded before he could even call for help.

Letting out a deep sigh, Mark turned and moved back into the small ship's main salon to pour himself a drink. They'd be back at the pier in less than an hour. He planned to have his men begin questioning the small community of dockworkers about strangers, but he was sure no one was going to admit seeing anyone lurking around his boat. He'd just have to play smarter now that he knew he'd underestimated the men of the Prairie Winds Club.

Chapter Sixteen

REGI HAD FORGOTTEN how exhausting diving could be and by the fifth day she felt like she'd been run through a wringer. The recovery team the Wests had hired were doing a great job, they were professional, conscientious, and she'd enjoyed diving with them. Regi had been impressed with how much they'd managed to bring up already, but there was something niggling in the back of her mind about the way the site had looked the last two days when they'd first gone down. It was as if someone had moved things ever so slightly. She'd shown a couple members of the team the markers she'd put in place and asked them to check them first thing. They had handheld communication units and could easily tap out a message to let her know whether or not things had been disturbed.

She'd planned to stay on top today and give her body a chance to recharge. Brian and Kirk had both expressed their concerns also and had threatened to lock her in their hotel suite if she didn't start taking better care of herself. Regi hadn't even gone to dinner with the rest of the Prairie Winds crew the night before, and anytime she preferred sleep to a good meal, it was sure sign she had overextended herself.

Lilly had finally passed her novice certification and would be making her first dive today. Regi had wanted to accompany her the first time down to the site, but she was fairly sure she wouldn't be able to persuade Lilly to wait until tomorrow. When Lilly West got something in her head she was a steamroller. Both her husbands had taken the class with her and promised Regi they'd take plenty of pictures. The older woman's eyes had been dancing with a mixture of excitement and wariness as she'd looked from her husbands to Regi while she'd donned her equipment. Just as Lilly slipped beneath the waves Regi had a flash of memory too fleeting to completely comprehend…all that had been left behind was an impression.

As she moved back up to the boat's deck, Regi mulled over what had just happened. Staring out over the water, she wondered what had been the catalyst for the memory. Then she remembered the way Lilly's eyes had moved between her and the West men, and Regi instantly re-membered there had been something *off* between her parents that day, and since tension had been so rare between them she had noticed. Regi's mom had been tired and mentioned several times that she was ready to go back to shore. They'd stayed longer at her dad's insistence and Regi remembered having the sense that her mom wasn't "on board" with whatever her husband had planned.

Standing at the portside rail, Regi noticed a much larg-er vessel clearly in view, but anchored a distance away. Regi hadn't seen any other boats earlier and she wondered how this one had managed to get so close without anyone noticing. Reaching for the high-powered monocular sitting on a nearby table, she focused in on the people moving on the wide diving platform. There was something about one of the divers…something so familiar she was barely breathing for fear he might disappear. Over the years she'd seen a number of people who had reminded her of her dad and her counselors had assured her it was a perfectly normal reaction to losing a loved one. But this man…oh this man moved with the exact fluid grace her father had. Her mother had often teased him that he'd been a dancer in his first life and he had usually swept her into his arms and waltzed her around the room to show her he still remembered the skills.

Regi watched as he touched his ear, a move she'd seen the men at Prairie Winds make when they were using the small communication devices the former Special Forces operatives seemed to favor. She tried not to think too much about the implications of that, when he raised his eyes and appeared to be looking directly at her, Regi felt as if all the air had suddenly been sucked from her lungs. As the divers slipped in to the water, she saw the telltale ripples from an underwater propeller and knew instinctively where the other ship's divers were headed.

MARK STEPHANO HADN'T planned to dive today until he'd listened to the taped conversation between Regina and the professionals the Wests had hired. Charlie had been right when he'd described her as intuitive as well as brilliant. *Definitely her mother's daughter.* She'd noticed the subtle changes in the site even though he and his men had taken great care to conceal their tampering. The current was strong enough that it was easy to hide the fact they'd taken several baskets of gold bars because there had been so many aboard the small ship it was natural for the sediment to shift with even the slightest movement of the water. But it was much harder to hide his search for the gold statues and large cache of gemstones that was reported to have been stored in the Captain's cabin rather than the ship's large cargo hold.

When Mark heard Regina say she wasn't diving today, he'd decided it was time to make a move. He'd made it clear to the other men accompanying that they were to frighten off the other team using as much intimidation as necessary. Mark had done his homework and knew Dean and Dell West would move their spirited wife out of harm's way at the first sign of trouble so he wasn't worried about hurting her. It wasn't that he considered Mrs. West an "innocent" *per se*. Hell, he'd read the reports and knew about her affinity for weapons and her lack of hesitation in using them. But he also knew Lilly West had taken a personal interest in Regina, becoming something close to a mother-figure during the past couple of years, and that went a long way ensuring her safety as far as he was concerned.

Moving quickly toward the site of the downed ship, Mark felt himself slip back into what his sweet wife had always called his "treasure hunter zone". He hadn't been able to argue with her because he'd always known his focus became incredibly narrow when he was diving. Even though he could chalk it up to safety concerns, he knew it was more than that…it was an adrenaline rush to feel a personal connection to history. Holding an artifact in his hand that had been crafted by someone centuries earlier was unlike anything else in the world, and it was a feeling he craved like a drug. *Ten years…I've stayed away from this for ten long years and I'm not sure I'll be able to live without it again.*

KIRK EVANS HAD reluctantly stayed behind when the others

left for the boat before dawn. He'd been up most of the night working to help one of their new partners deal with a particularly difficult patient. After several days at sea, Kirk was in desperate need of some downtime on land. He loved spending time with Regi and he'd tried desperately to convince her to stay at the hotel with him, but she'd laughed and told him they *both* knew he wouldn't get any rest if she stayed. He hated knowing she was nearly as depleted as he was, but the most he'd managed to get her to concede was that she wouldn't dive today.

Leaning back against the bed's intricately carved headboard, he tried to close his eyes and will his body to take advantage of the opportunity for rest. But the temptation to fall head first into the memories of the past month proved too sweet to resist. The McCall's wedding seemed to set everything in motion and it was fitting when he considered the incredible energy that appeared to follow Jen McCall. Kirk was grateful Regi had developed close friendships with the other women at the Prairie Winds Club because it was obvious a decade spent trying to fly under the radar after her parents' strange deaths had hindered Regi's ability to form long-lasting friendships. Seeing to her safety and happiness were quickly becoming his number one priority. He and Brian had already contacted the jeweler recommended by Kyle and Kent West, and given him the go-ahead to begin designing an engagement ring for Regi.

Kirk smiled to himself as he remembered how his concerns they were rushing things had been put to rest very early this morning. He'd taken a short break from the phone at three a.m. and returned to their room to check on Regi. As soon as he opened the bedroom door he'd seen her standing on the balcony. With the soft glow of the street lamps shimmering over her skin and washing over the ivory silk chemise she was wearing, he'd just watched her for several long seconds. She looked like a sexy angel standing beneath the stars and he'd relished the chance to study her as she looked out over the soft white caps of the Caribbean Sea. Her long hair had been perfectly tousled and falling over her shoulders in gentle waves of auburn wonder. She was staring out over the rippling water as if she'd find the answer to all the Universe's deepest questions written in the turbulent tide. In repose, the classic lines of her beauty stole his breath, but it was the come-hither smile when she noticed him watching her that had shaken him to the depths of his soul.

Stepping up behind her so he could wrap her in the shelter of his arms, he'd kissed the top of her head and inhaled the sweet scent of her citrus shampoo. "You smell sweet enough to eat, *anoshi*. What weighs so heavily on your mind it has you standing out here exposed to the dangers of the world?" He'd wanted her to understand his concern for her safety, but he hadn't wanted the conversation to become adversarial either. The warrior in his ancestry and the sexual Dominant in his personality wanted to demand she take every precaution possible. He was also completely captivated by the miracle of the woman in his arms, and right now he sensed that was the side of him she needed most.

Regi had turned in his embrace, wrapping her arms around his waist and rested her cheek against his chest. Feeling her press herself against him was pure magic and they had stayed that way for long minutes. When he finally slid his hand slowly up her back to cradle the base of her skull in his palm, she'd tipped her head back into his palm letting him hold her perfectly in place as he leaned down to capture her mouth in a kiss that was a conversation of love between their spirits. He'd leisurely explored every recess of her mouth and felt the groan of satisfaction bubble up in the back of his throat when her body went lax in surrender.

The silk nightgown she was wearing barely hid the bottom curves of her ass cheeks and he easily slid his fingers into the small gap just beneath the slick folds of her sex. Kirk loved the way Regi's body responded to his and Brian's touch. As soon as his fingers brushed over her cream soaked labia she instinctively moved her legs further apart giving him unimpeded access to her sex. He'd slid just the tip of his middle finger into her channel and felt her internal muscles rippling as they tried to pull him deeper. Her desire was quickly becoming an addiction, and for the first time in his life, Kirk truly understood how difficult it was for those lost in the darkness of chemical addictions to avoid the lure of a drug's siren call.

His low-riding cotton shorts were doing nothing to hide his body's reaction and he didn't care. When he picked her up she wrapped her legs around his waist and he could feel the heat from her pussy settle against his throbbing erection. "I want you. In this moment there is nothing I want more than to feel your body wrapped around my cock. My fingers are coated with your sweet syrup and knowing your body is ready for me is one of the biggest turn-ons in the world." Regi hadn't responded with words, but the shudder he felt quake through her was all the encouragement he needed. Pushing the barrier aside freeing his cock in one deft move, he felt her heat surround him as he pushed into her. "Perfect. Your body is scorching and so fucking perfect that it humbles me to know men from all eternity have experienced this same rapture."

It amazed him that people traveled thousands of miles

to walk along the paths of their ancestors when all they had to do was love another person to share something their forefathers had experienced. Before Regi, sex had been little more than a physical release, but with her, it was so much more. He'd cupped her ass cheeks in his palms and begun lifting her so she slid up and down his shaft.

"So good…oh God, it's so amazing. I can feel each ridge of your cock caressing me from the inside and the ridges send me into orbit. It's as if your body was made just for me. I can't think for the pleasure rolling over me in waves threatening to pull me under and claim me as their own." Kirk wasn't even sure Regi realized she was speaking aloud as her mind lost itself in the sweet rapture of her body's response. If he had his way, he wouldn't let her surface from the bliss for hours, but he knew his body wasn't going to hold off that long because it was already chasing a mind numbing release.

Kirk didn't even try to capture her sweet moans and cries as the orgasm claimed her. He hadn't been strong enough to hold out against the onslaught of a soul stealing pleasure and he had quickly followed her over the edge. The explosion of light behind his eyelids rivaled the most brilliant fireworks displays he'd ever seen and the only thing that kept him from collapsing into a heap was the fact he'd locked his knees and grasped the balcony's railing.

"Are you alright, *mi amõre*? That was a bit more frenzied that I would have liked, but you just undo me. The moment your body took flight, I couldn't help but follow you." He'd known his voice sounded as if he'd just run a marathon and in the back of his mind he noted the comparison was probably fairly accurate.

"Mmmm, I'd have to say I'm much better than alright." Kirk's connection to Regi was strengthening to the point he could often feel her emotions as if they were his own. He could feel her floating in the sweet bliss of afterglow, her body was sated even though she was quickly falling over the edge of exhaustion. When his body slipped from hers, he was nearly overcome by an odd sense of male satisfaction when he felt his cum trailing down the insides of her thighs. After resettling his shorts around his waist, he scooped her up in his arms and moved to the bathroom to help her clean up. After patting her dry, he'd settled her back in bed so he could return to the den. She'd been sleeping soundly as he'd pulled the sheet over her. Brian had smiled up at him and then gathered her into his arms as Kirk pulled the door closed behind him.

Now, as he reclined on the bed where he'd laid her just a few hours ago, Kirk pulled her pillow against his face and inhaled. He could still smell the faintest hint of her and it let him slip slowly into sleep.

Chapter Seventeen

REGI WAS CONVINCED the divers from the other boat she'd watched slip into the sparkling blue water of the Caribbean Sea were heading for the ship wreck she and her crew had been recovering for the past several days. Moving quickly to the equipment storage area, she immediately started pulling on her wetsuit. When the recovery team's dive master stepped in front of her intent on halting her progress, Regi wanted to growl with frustration. "You said you were not diving today. What are you doing?" He was obviously not pleased with her change of plans and she knew if she didn't appease him, she wouldn't get the tanks she'd need to make the dive.

"I need to go down. I just watched several divers from another boat go into the water and I am sure they are headed this way." She'd tried to keep her tone even despite her growing unease. She had waved her hand in the general direction of the other vessel, but hadn't actually looked at the man she was speaking to so she didn't know if he'd taken notice of the boat of not. Continuing to pull on her dive suit, she finally added, "Look, I know I'd said I wasn't diving today, but something about this just doesn't feel right to me. Don't you ever just *know* that something is wrong?" Regi had no more than spoken the words than she felt Brian's strong arms encircle her waist and pull her back against his bare chest.

"Regi...stop for a minute." Brian's voice was soft, but the command was unmistakable. "What's going on, baby? Can you tell us why you think the divers are headed this direction?" The words were spoken with a level of calm that didn't match the firm way he was holding her and Regi knew he'd picked up her rising panic. His arms banded her close, halting her movements and Regi cursed her body's immediate reaction to even that small bit of bondage. Her heartbeat sped up for an entirely new reason and she immediately felt the moisture dampening her sex. *Damn my traitorous body.* Regi had played with other Doms while working at the club, but she had rarely had sex with them, because she'd never felt any real *connection* to them. But things had been different with both Brian and Kirk from the first time they'd met, and despite her best efforts to keep them at arm's length, the chemistry between them was just too much to fight. Regi felt some of the fear that she'd been feeling leach from her body as she took a couple of deep breaths.

Squirming to turn so she could step back out of his embrace and look up into his eyes, she smiled when he wrapped his hand around her wrist with his fingers pressing against her pulse point. *Damned doctor doesn't think I know what he's doing? As if it isn't enough he's a Dom and can read every nuance of my body, but now he's going to play the doctor card?*

She was grateful he'd pushed his sunglasses up so she could better see his reactions to what she was going to tell him. She knew Kirk would understand if she just said she *knew without knowing how she knew.* But Brian wasn't an empath and he was going to expect her to give him a very good reason for diving when he didn't think it was in her best interest. "I watched them for a few minutes before they went into the water. One of the divers looked right at me so I know they were watching our boat as well." She took another steadying breath, "There was something so familiar about the way the man moved...I can't explain it, but I know him. And if I know him, then we have a problem. I also recognize the signs of a hand-held underwater propeller. They are using them and they're headed this way."

Regi waited for what seemed an eternity while Brian mulled over her words. She'd just about given up on getting a response from him when he nodded once and released her wrist. He immediately started barking orders to the people who had gathered around them. The dive master hadn't questioned Brian's decision like he had hers and Regi wasn't sure if it was because he'd been satisfied with her explanation or because his orders were now coming from a man. She tried not to think about that too much, but did make a note to mention it to Lilly West...hell, it was worth the entertainment alone to watch her friend work when she thought any of "her girls" were being treated as second-class citizens. The interrogation Lilly would subject him to would probably be enough to have the man jumping overboard.

KYLE WEST LAID the sheaf of papers he'd been reading down on his desk and looked across the gleaming mahogany surface at his twin who was studying him carefully. The police report on Charlie Hendricks' death left no question that he'd been murdered and it appeared it was something he had expected. Kent cleared his throat and spoke, "Obviously Hendricks knew Stephano was still alive and expected him to visit. Hell, five cameras in the room was overkill even by *our* standards. What I don't understand is why he didn't tell Regi. Why let her mourn the loss of her parents if they weren't really gone, unless Mark was up to his ass in alligators and hiding was the only thing that could save them."

"I don't know. I haven't sorted it out yet, but I don't believe in coincidences. And since Stephano already knows we have a team in Belize, he may well make a move on Regi, and that means none of our people are safe." Kyle was suddenly terrified for his family and friends.

"Agreed. We need to make calls immediately. They need to be warned and I want them headed in this direction immediately. Hell, their rooms aren't even safe at this point." Just as Kent finished speaking, he looked up to see Tobi standing in the doorway. She'd been busy bringing the new nanny up to speed when they'd come downstairs a few minutes ago and they'd given her explicit instructions to rest once the young woman they'd hired was comfortable. She looked exhausted, pale, terrified, and more beautiful than he could ever remember. It didn't matter that she was wearing faded jeans that looked like they were barely hanging on her slender hips and a baggy sweatshirt that one of their babies had taken the liberty of decorating with something he was sure wasn't worth mentioning. Kent simply raised his outstretched hand to her and smiled as he watched her move to him without hesitation. After settling her on his lap, Kent looked down at her and asked, "Why aren't you resting? I thought our instructions were pretty clear."

She dug in her pocket and pulled out his phone. "It had been ringing continually, but the only call I answered was Kirk's. He wanted you to know that he'd stayed behind today and had been so uneasy that he'd started looking around their suite. He found several devices he is sure are bugs. He's going to send you the pictures and I thought you would want to know about this right away." Just then his phone dinged notifying him that he had a new message.

She leaned forward and looked at the screen with him and he had to bite back a grin when she whistled. "I recognize one of those, I saw Micah working on one like it the other day. He swore it was for one of the private rooms upstairs, but I'm betting a curtsy on a cactus he uses it in the gazebo." The tone of voice alone told him that she hadn't bought Micah's excuse and Kent worked hard to suppress his laughter at the wager she'd mentioned.

Tobi and her friends loved the large white gazebo down by the edge of the river. It was their favored location for most of their get-togethers and it was more likely than not exactly where the head of their security team was planning to put the state of the art device. He and Kyle both tried not to laugh at their insightful bundle of trouble as they reminded her that she shouldn't question the honestly of one of their employees, even in jest without a good reason. Kent loved Tobi the moment she'd come out of Kyle's truck the day they'd met, and just when he thought he couldn't love her anymore, he realized he did.

No one said anything for a several seconds, but Kyle finally broke the silence. "Why don't you go back up and rest for a while. Leave your clothes in our room, but then go up to the roof. We've made a few improvements and think you're going to enjoy them." The patio area was one of her favorite places at Prairie Winds and it had been Kyle's special project when they'd first purchased the property. His brother hadn't cared much about the interior design of their large living space on the top floor, but he'd planned each and every detail of the roof's tropical paradise design.

Kent already knew she wouldn't go—not until she knew her friends and family members were safe. Loyalty ran bone-deep in their woman and Kent certainly couldn't find any fault in that trait. He also knew Kyle hadn't expected she would do as he'd asked either, but Kent knew his twin had felt obligated to try because everything about her was practically screaming an impending collapse from fatigue. She looked at each of them and then slowly shook her head, "You know I can't do that…even though I want to more than I care to admit. But I won't be able to rest until I know all of our family and friends are safe." It was exactly what Kent had expected and obviously Kyle hadn't been surprised either because he simply nodded. She gave them both a small grin and her eyes regained a small spark, "Alrighty then…how can I help so we can all go up to the roof together?"

Kent was thrilled to hear her offer to help, because truthfully she was resourceful and organized. She might not have the specialized contacts they had on speed dial, but she'd be able to call their team members and make sure they knew what was coming down. The three of them split up and began calling each of their people, leaving messages and alerting the local law enforcement officials to the problem. Kirk was already on his way to the pier, so Kent secured a speedboat that would be ready and waiting by the time he arrived. He'd listened to Tobi leave increasingly alarmed messages on both of his dads' phones and by the time he knew she was dialing his mom's number he'd gently taken the phone from her hands and left the message for her himself.

Tobi and his mom had become extremely close, and he

didn't want both women operating from a position of panic. Kent knew if Tobi left a hysterical message for Lilly West, the woman would move heaven and hell to get home without any concern for her own safety along the way. In less than an hour they'd made all the calls they could and now the hard part would begin. Waiting had never been easy for him and Kent knew it was an even bigger challenge for Kyle. As Navy SEALs, they'd learned the value of patience during missions but those had never involved their parents or close friends, so Kent worried it was going to be a long few hours until they knew how things were going. Patience was in no way their sweet wife's strong suit either, so distraction was certainly going to be in order—and lucky for her that was something he and his brother excelled at.

Chapter Eighteen

REGI AND BRIAN slipped beneath the surface and quickly made their way to the wreck. Lilly West was the first person she looked for and she'd been very easy to spot because her husbands were flanking her. While Lilly looked at the site, Dean and Dell watched her. Regi had always envied their relationship and despite her concern for Lilly's safety, she still found herself biting back a smile when she saw one of the men slide his hand up the back of his wife's thigh and cup her ass cheek. Just as she and Brian reached the group, she saw the intruders move forward out of the shadows. There were several of them, but the one that drew her eye was just behind the first man to move into her field of vision. Regi positioned herself between the newcomers and Lilly and wasn't surprised to see Brian move in front of her.

There wasn't any doubt why the men were there, their hand signals were crystal clear. They intended to take over the site and were ordering the others back. Regi moved forward giving the newcomers the signal for claimed site. They answered by raising their weapons in her direction. When they'd first decided to return to the wreck site, Regi had started researching weapons that could be fired safely underwater, and she'd been surprised to learn there weren't many. A few handguns and even fewer rifles, and those were usually only made available to members of law enforcement and the military. She doubted these men were anything more than thieves, but she wasn't confident enough to test the theory that their weapons would harm the shooter more than the target if fired underwater.

The man Regi knew was the leader put his hand on the arm of the man in front of him and Regi watched as the weapon slowly lowered. Regi felt as if she was being drawn forward by some magnetic field. The second man hadn't taken his eyes off her and she now focused on him. She knew those eyes, but her mind refused to accept what was so glaringly clear. She felt herself starting to shake and knew her reaction wouldn't be missed by the other members of her dive team. Her mouth went dry, tears filled her eyes, and in the next second the icy stab of betrayal shook her to her core. *How? Why? You disappear from my life and only reappear because I've figured out the location of your gold?* Her eyes moved as she began tracking the other members of the group searching for her mom. When she returned her gaze to her dad, she could see the overwhelming sadness in his dark eyes and knew she was really gone.

Regi hadn't done much diving since that day with her parents, but she'd never forgotten her dad's hand signals, so when she saw him sign for her to return topside she quickly shook her head. When he repeated the sign and then swept his arm to draw her attention to the armed men surrounding him, she once again shook her head. This time his hand signal told her that she was in danger, and she'd finally recovered enough to feel the shock of betrayal begin to change into something that was much closer to rage. She gave a hard kick to propel herself forward breaking Brian's hold on her upper arm. She saw the man just in front of her dad raise his weapon and then it felt as if her head exploded as he hit her with the butt of the gun. In the time it took her to blink, chaos ensued.

Dex Raines and Ash Moore moved faster underwater than Regi had ever imagined possible, obviously their BUD/S training and years spent as Navy SEALs had served them well. She felt herself being shoved back and just as her vision cleared she heard the explosion of a gun being fired. The compression slammed against her chest, making her feel as if she'd been hit with a cannonball, and for an instant she worried she'd actually been shot. But the blood coming from Brian's shoulder told her who had taken the bullet. He'd put himself between her and the man who was obviously acting as her father's bodyguard and had been shot in the process.

There was confusion all around her but the only thing Regi could focus on was the fact Brian Bennett had been shot trying to protect her. She watched as one of Lilly's husbands moved her quickly toward the surface and the other stayed behind moving into place to help surround her. All of the struggling was kicking up sand and ocean floor debris to the point Regi was having trouble seeing more than a couple of feet in front of her. She was trying to press the heel of her hand against Brian's wound when she realized her swim fin and foot were caught under the shifting remains of the ship. They were much closer to the ledge than she ordinarily ventured and when everything started to shift, she felt fear mushroom as she struggled to free her leg. In the span of a few seconds she'd gone from angry that poachers were moving in…to devastated when she realized the last decade of her life had been a lie…to terrified that she was going to be pulled into an underwater crevice with very little hope for survival.

MARK COULDN'T BELIEVE his eyes when he met Regina's gaze. She'd recognized him immediately and he'd seen her go from disbelief to hurt to angry in less than a minute. When he'd told her to go back to the surface he'd seen the slight upward tilt of her chin and it had reminded him so much of her mother he'd been forced to bite back a smile. But his amusement had been short-lived. He saw her legs move to kick forward and his guard had seen the move as an act of aggression and quickly slammed the butt of his Glock against the side of her head. What followed was like watching a disaster unfold right in front of him. Everything had taken mere seconds but seemed to play out like a slow motion movie reel he couldn't stop. The man who had been by Regina's side moved in front of her just as the weapon fired. *Hell, the noise alone was enough to make me never want to be near another gun.* And the concussion of sound was so strong it felt like getting kicked in the chest.

What followed could only be described as complete and utter pandemonium. A part of him had expected the Three Stooges to appear because everything that could go wrong did—and so quickly it was if the entire scene had been scripted as the clusterfuck to end all clusterfucks. There were people all around him jockeying for position, but all Mark could focus on was his only child frantically trying to free her leg from the wreckage that was teetering precariously close to the edge of a crevice. When he tried to move to help her the men guarding her blocked him. The only one who wasn't standing with his back to her completely oblivious to her predicament, had just been shot and was rapidly losing consciousness.

Mark watched as the beams holding her foot shifted and Regina was thrown away from the injured diver she had been frantically helping. He saw her eyes go wide as she was pushed closer and closer to the lip of the ravine. All of the movement was causing the water around them to churn and Mark knew it was only a matter of time before the entire wreck tumbled out of sight. And when that happened, anyone close would be sucked down with it by the force of the water rushing around them. The ridge was deeper than any other in the area, that was one of the reasons the wreck had not been discovered sooner. The locals had passed down tales for generations about the magnetic pull of the sea demon residing in the depths of the rift. The demon was said to pull unsuspecting ships and divers to their deaths when they ventured too close.

He'd heard all the folklore and long considered the stories to work in his favor because they kept the local divers from moving in on his find, but suddenly those harrowing tales were beginning to seem all too real. He was quickly losing patience with the men surrounding Regina and had just decided he might have to shoot one of them in order to help her when the largest man finally glanced over his shoulder.

Mark gave his men a quick sign indicating she was his daughter and the change in their focus was immediate. Once everyone knew Regina was in trouble, all attention shifted to her. One of the men Mark recognized as Dean West pulled the injured diver back and started to the surface despite the man's vehement protests. The largest of the divers who had been guarding Regi pulled an enormous knife from a sheath and began cutting the fin as quickly as he could without hurting Regina. Her ankle was still wedged tight, but she'd have a better chance of wiggling free without the added length of her swim fin. Mark knew she was using up her tank at an alarming rate because he could see the rapid rise and fall of her chest. Panic breathing would burn up her air quickly if she didn't calm down.

Bringing her attention to him, he signaled for her to breathe slower and look at him, not what the men were doing. He saw her eyes fill with tears but she nodded even as she tried to wave him back, indicating she wanted him to move aside to safety. Why she would care about his safety after all he'd done was a mystery to him, but it confirmed what an amazing young woman she'd grown into. The crushing weight of all he'd missed…the milestones in her life that he hadn't shared with her…the lost opportunities to just spend an afternoon walking along the beach talking…the realization of what he'd done sent a stab of regret straight through his heart.

Mark kept checking Regina's regulator and was becoming increasingly alarmed at how quickly her tank was being depleted. He knew they were close to freeing her but no one seemed to be watching how unstable the wreckage was and he worried they were all going to be pulled over the edge if they didn't move away immediately. As he helped move aside a large beam his foot brushed against the surface moving aside a large piece of what looked like the remains of a chest. The hinges and clasp looked like they'd been handcrafted—their ornate designs were definitely Mayan. But it was the glimmering gold beneath that stole his breath. For several seconds he was too shocked to even move. Reaching for the largest piece, he noted the green, black, and purple jade favored by Mayan royalty. The piece was heavy and sparkled even in the dim light. The last report of its existence was in the archives of the Temple of Inscriptions, but the stories of its mystical powers were the stuff of legends and had been passed down for generations. He'd never believed in anything he couldn't prove, but the surge of power he felt when his fingers wrapped around one of the larger stones was undeniable.

Mark felt a surge of pure energy that was almost hypnotic in its intensity. Looking at the colored stones was like falling into a churning sea of pure color, pulling him deeper and deeper into its hold. It was only when one of his men grabbed his shoulder that he managed to pull himself back to the moment. It was frightening to think about how mesmerized he'd been just looking at something the ancients had believed held the power to persuade kings to give away their entire kingdoms. Returning quickly to Regi's side, he managed to slip it over her head and see the look of absolute wonder in her eyes. Her leg came free and the men who had been helping her quickly moved her toward the surface. He saw her glance back at him just as everything around him started to swirl and he was caught in a powerful whirlpool, pulling him into the black abyss.

Chapter Nineteen

R EGI LOOKED DOWN at the heavy piece her dad had put around her neck and knew instantly what it was. She was bowled over to know the myths and legends about a magical necklace belonging to a Mayan Queen were true—and she'd felt the power of the stones almost immediately. The only way she would ever be able to describe it was to compare it to being suddenly *plugged into and finely tuned to* some kind of universal power. She'd pulled her leg free and felt her breathing slow immediately. Ash and Dex had been sharing their air with her for the past several minutes after her tank had depleted quickly. She was grateful for their expertise because she doubted she would have made it without their unruffled guidance.

She'd been very grateful when Dean had taken Brian back to the surface, but she had missed his calming presence. Looking back to make sure her dad was following them to the surface, Regi was horrified by what she saw. Watching the swirl of water sucking the wreckage over the edge of the chasm was sad enough, but seeing the other divers fighting futilely for their lives as they tried to escape. The scene playing out below her was the most horrifying thing she had ever witnessed. She found her dad quickly and gasped when she realized he wasn't going to make it. He looked up locking gazes with her and quickly placed his fist over his heart giving her their sign for *I love you* before disappearing into the black depths.

Ash had turned her face to his own and had shaken his head vigorously, letting her know there wasn't anything they could do even as they continued slowly making their way to the surface. Regi's mind had gone completely numb. *How can I live through losing him again?* Somewhere in the back of her mind, she realized the high-pitched buzzing sound was the whine of a speedboat as it closed in on them quickly, but she was so lost in her sorrow she hadn't even taken time to question who would be approaching so quickly.

When they finally reached the surface, Regi pushed her mask from her face and took gulping breaths of fresh air as sobs wracked her body. She felt strong hands wrap around her upper arms and lift her effortlessly from the water an instant before Kirk pulled her against his chest. His arms felt like bands of steel as he locked her in his embrace. "Oh my Gods and Goddess, *anoshi*, I thought I would never see you again." Regi had never felt such anguish coming from another person and for a moment she realized he was feeling the same emotions from her.

As soon as the men had removed her diving equipment, Kirk bent over and easily scooped her into his arms and moved to the deck. He settled in a quiet corner and just rocked her until she'd finally settled enough to pull back and look up at him. It had taken her several minutes to bring herself back under control enough to ask about Brian and tell Kirk what she'd seen. Before she'd finished, she heard the unmistakable thumping of helicopter blades and looked up in horror as it neared their position. "It's alright, they are transporting Brian for assessment and treatment. His injury isn't life threatening, but he *has* lost a lot of blood and the risk of infection is huge so it's important to get him to shore as quickly as possible." She saw a shadow of amusement skate over his features for just a second before he added, "You know it's amazing to watch how quickly Dell West can go from good ole Texas boy to tyrannical shipping billionaire. He is a sight to behold when he wants something done. I'm sure there is a lesson in there somewhere, but I'm going to have to table that for now."

"Are you going with Brian?" She hated how shaky her voice had sounded knowing he'd never leave her side unless he was convinced she was settled.

"No, *anoshi*. I'm not leaving your side again. I would consider it a mistake that I did so earlier today, except it gave me the opportunity to find the listening devices in our suite. I only wish I'd found them sooner." She could see the regret in his eye and hated the fact he felt like he'd let everyone down.

Moving to shift closer, Regi pressed her lips to his and wrapped her arms around him. "There was no way to know how tangled this was." *Hell, I need a map and it's my life. I swear I would write a book but it would piss me off when they classified it as fiction.* "Now you see why I was so reluctant to become involved with you and Brian. It wasn't that I wasn't interested. I was afraid I'd have to move on and it's so much harder when there are people in your life who matter." She felt her eyes fill with tears and had to take several deep breaths to hold them back. "Can we head in to the hospital now? I'm worried about Brian and I don't like the idea of him being there alone."

Kirk grinned, "We are all heading to the hospital and Dean West is flying with Brian, much to the pilot's derision. We'll go right away but we won't take the speedboat…Dex and Ash have called dibs on that. They are adamant they need it so they can secure the hospital, but I feel quite certain Kyle and Kent have already handled that." He chuckled, "They don't fool me, those two adrenaline junkies see the opportunity for a near death adventure and they're all over it." When Regi rolled her eyes she felt everything in Kirk's demeanor change in a heartbeat and her entire body went on alert. He leaned close and whispered against her ear, "Be very careful rolling your eyes at your Master, my sweet little subbie. There are some rules that are hard-and-fast with swift repercussions in our world. Something to keep in mind as your nearly bare ass is ever so close to my palm." His palm gripped her bikini-clad bottom and a shiver raced up her spine.

Regi felt her pussy moisten and her nipples tighten in response to the change in Kirk. It was only then that she realized the helicopter had taken off and they were moving. The boat was picking up speed and the deck wasn't going to be the most comfortable place to ride out their fast trip back to shore. Kirk set her on her feet and led her to the lower level cabin they'd been using earlier. "Let's get the salt water washed off you and then I think a remedial session about protocol is in order. It seems as though you've been away from the club too long, *anoshi*."

Feeling herself slip into the familiar submissive mindset grounded her as Kirk would have known it would. She was grateful he'd taken the initiative to bring her scattered thoughts back into some semblance of order. The part of being a submissive that had always appealed to Regi the most was the freedom she knew could be found when you didn't have to worry about making any of the decisions. Everything about her life outside of the scenes she had participated in at the club required her to stay in total control and to make life and death decisions in the time it took most people to blink a problem into focus.

Submitting to Kirk and Brian was soul shattering in its intensity each time they came together and raw power had intimidated her in the beginning. She knew the deep connection she felt with them had started with her seeing them as a unit. Everything had always centered around them together and their time had been limited to the rare occasions they could all play at the club. But over time that link had morphed into something so much deeper and extended to them as individuals as they'd all become friends in addition to D/s play partners. Since she'd been staying with them, Regi had realized how they each brought something different into her life and now she found it almost impossible to imagine how empty her life would be if they decided to end their time with her. Her sudden melancholy wasn't missed and Kirk cupped each side of her face so her attention was focused on him, "What was that thought, Regi? And don't even think about lying or glossing over it because I *will* know if you try."

His words hadn't been particularly harsh, but she'd certainly felt the steel threaded through the command. She didn't doubt that he would indeed know if her answer wasn't completely transparent. But she wasn't sure she could bare her soul when she was already reeling from the day's events. She'd spent a decade hiding behind a carefully constructed persona as a bold and out-spoken woman who didn't need anyone's approval, so suddenly letting some-one see how vulnerable she felt was terrifying.

KIRK KNEW REGI was on an emotional roller coaster, he also knew she wasn't going to be able to pull herself back from the edge without help. One of the things he'd learned about intelligent, successful women was they often struggled to yield the personal power they fought so hard for in the workplace. However, when they were able to trust enough to "let go", the freedom they found made it worth the effort. He and Brian had always been convinced you could learn as much or more about being a Sexual Dominant during aftercare as you could during classes— and at Prairie Winds that was saying a lot, because the classes for both Doms and subs at Prairie Winds were the most thorough Kirk had ever seen. They not only covered all of the reasons *Safe, Sane, and Consensual* was the guiding tenant, but the continuing education gave both groups in depth training on the huge spectrum of lifestyle choices recognized at the club. The goal was to keep everyone safe and Kirk admired their success because there were rarely any injuries requiring medical care and he'd never seen one that required outside intervention.

The Wests had always stressed the importance of aftercare and it was during those moments, when a sub was often at her most vulnerable. He and Brian had observed varying versions of the same challenge, but basically it had boiled down to how difficult it was for many subs to learn how to *let go*. But the women they'd talked to had unanimously agreed that the peace they felt once they discovered the freedom found in submitting had been a refuge they sought regularly.

Kirk didn't doubt for a moment that Regi's personal life had added an additional layer of difficulty to her ability to put herself totally in another's hands. He also suspected she was worried the baggage she claimed to be carrying would eventually be too much for them to handle. "You are over thinking this, *anoshi*. It really isn't at all difficult. Just answer honestly." He was sure she hadn't even realized she was crying until he leaned forward and kissed her tears away with gentle brushes of his lips. "If you think you will hurt my feelings, let me assure you that I can only think of two ways for you to do that—by leaving or lying. The only two things that will hurt me. Everything else just *is*. We'll always have issues to work through, sweetheart. Every couple has their challenges, and ménage couples face some that are particularly interesting at times."

He gave her a few seconds to take in what he'd said before adding, "I'm sure you know Lilly, Tobi, and Gracie have all been confronted in public for their decision to live a ménage lifestyle. And I know all three of those ladies are very capable of taking care of themselves and speaking their minds, but I also know words can be used as weapons and they do their damage no matter how strong the target is."

She undoes me. When I touch her, it is as if her heart is speaking to mine. Looking into her eyes was almost a spiritual experience at times because her soul was so clearly reflected there. Her emotions played out right in front of him and Kirk tried to keep his own emotions in check. He knew if she picked up on his frustration or anxiety she would lock her feelings away from him no matter what the consequences.

"Let me see if I can help. You are worried everything that has happened will in some way convince us you aren't worth the trouble and we'll move on to someone *less complicated*. Is that about it?" Regi studied his face for long moments wondering how he'd known...how he'd managed to see it so clearly. She also watched to see if he was sincere or mocking because there wasn't much she hated more than being made fun of when she felt vulnerable.

Letting out the breath she'd been holding, Regi sighed in relief when she saw nothing but honestly reflecting in his onyx eyes. Regi finally managed to nod because she couldn't speak around the knot in her throat. She felt tears streaming down her cheeks and she was grateful that Kirk didn't try to diminish her feelings by telling her everything would be alright. He just let her vent the emotion in the only way she could.

It didn't take long for her to realize what a terrible waste of time her tears were and she was relieved he didn't protest when she suddenly pulled back. He just smiled, "Welcome back, Regi. I knew that feisty woman was in there somewhere." She could only blink at him because he'd surprised her again by reading her mood so perfectly. "Don't look so surprised, love, I really do know you far better than you realize. Now, let's get cleaned up and dressed. I want to be ready to head out as soon as we dock." When she just stood looking at him, he winked, "I know you were expecting a spanking, but sometimes lessons are taught with denial." Regi couldn't hold back her giggle at his outrageous behavior even though she knew he'd made a sincere effort to lighten the moment, and she was truly grateful.

BOBBING IN THE wake of the large salvage boat, a lone figure watched quietly as it sped away. He hadn't bothered making any attempt to draw the crew's attention and had ducked down when the helicopter had lifted off the upper deck and raced toward the shore. Swimming back to his own boat would be arduous, but he had nothing but time. And if he became too tired, he'd simply wait until the other vessel was out of sight and then press the locator button on his watch. He knew the man he'd left on the boat wouldn't leave until he was absolutely certain no one was returning. And since Joey had no way of knowing every other member of the team had been lost, there wasn't much cause to worry about being abandoned.

Rolling over onto his back, he began leisurely making his way through the water, grateful the surface was much more cooperative than the floor had been. He'd lost several good men, but he wouldn't mourn the loss. They all knew the perils of working with him and he'd make sure their families were well taken care of. Smiling to himself, he sent up a silent prayer to the sweet guardian angel he knew had been responsible for today's turn of event. "Thank you, my sweet Nalia." He planned to take advantage of this second chance at a second chance. He hadn't been as wise the last time…but he wouldn't make the same mistakes this go-around.

Feeling oddly energized, he rolled over and pressed the button on his watch that would bring help. Mark could barely hold back his grin when he heard the motor start. *It's amazing how much freedom there is in dying…again!*

Epilogue

REGI STOOD IN the gazebo looking out over the river's sparkling water and counted her blessings. She was surrounded by people she loved and who loved her unconditionally in return. In her mind there wasn't much more you could hope for. She had read and reread the letter from Charlie until the edges of the paper had become tattered, but his words had mended a lot of the damage to her heart. The fractures she'd felt from his complicity and silence weren't completely healed, but knowing she had brought love into his life had gone a long way in renewing her faith in others.

The time she'd spent in Florida settling his estate had also helped bring things into perspective. Regi had been thrilled to learn Charlie had left his house and a large trust fund to his long-time housekeeper. Cecelia was a lovely woman and had obviously loved her boss very much. Regi had helped Cecelia find a financial planner that advised the middle-aged beauty on investments. Even with modest returns on the money, she would be able to live comfortably for the rest of her life without continuing the backbreaking work she'd been doing since she'd been a teenager.

When Regi first learned of the money Charlie had left for her, she'd been completely stunned, realizing the enormity of the gift. Her entire adult life had been spent struggling financially, so having so much wealth thrust upon her had been daunting in the beginning. The negotiations for the recovered treasures were progressing and that was going to be another windfall that she hadn't expected. She had recently been in contact with a woman who was in the early planning stages of a new women and children's wing for the medical center where Kirk and Brian were on staff. Regi planned to meet with Merilee D. Lanham later in the week to discuss making a large donation in Kirk and Brian's names.

Regi was also working to set up an education foundation to fund scholarships targeting students who found themselves in witness protection programs for whatever reason. Regi knew how lucky she'd been that Charlie had helped her navigate the system, and she wanted to repay that kindness the best way she knew how.

She felt Brian step up behind her before he actually touched her or spoke. Her connection with both men seemed to grow stronger every day. They had asked her to marry them several times and she'd always stalled for this reason or that. Now she could only hope they hadn't given up on her. She sighed in contentment as Brian wrapped his good arm around her and pulled her back against his warm chest. The air was finally starting to feel as though fall had arrived even though it seemed particularly late this year.

Brian's left arm was still in a sling from the latest surgery to remove the scar tissue, but this time the prognosis had been more encouraging than those they'd heard previously. As she'd feared, infection had been the biggest issue he'd faced, and they'd nearly lost him before his transfer from the hospital in Belize. The financial and political resources of the West and McCall families had played an enormous role in saving Brian's life, and Regi would always be grateful for everything they'd done.

"Where are you, my love? You look as if your thoughts are scattered in the wind." Brian always had a way of drawing her out of a funk. Even when he'd been delirious with the fevers that had ravaged his entire body, his first concern had always been her. It had frustrated her when he'd put his worry about her above his own health even as it had humbled her to see how easily the life she'd always wished for was within her grasp. She had only wanted to hold Brian and Kirk off on their marriage plans until things had settled down, but they hadn't mentioned it for several days and she was beginning to worry. If she was hon-est...she was as anxious as they were, but she had wanted to be able to fully enjoy everything being engaged entailed and that meant cutting down on the distractions now cluttering her mind.

"I was just counting my blessings." She paused just for a second hoping he could see how sincere she was, "I hope you know that having you here...on the road to recov-ery...is at the top of the list. You and Kirk are always going to share that top spot." It had taken her so long to admit how much they meant to her, but the words had finally tumbled out while he'd been lying in that ICU unit in Belize. And once she'd finally been able to get past the hurdle of admitting to them and to herself how much she wanted them both, Regi hadn't hesitated to repeat the words at every opportunity.

The afternoon sun was shining down on the water sending sparkles of light dancing over the surface, remind-ing Regi of the stories about fairies she'd read as a child. Her mother had always insisted those dancing lights were angels sent to honor the mysteries of the sea and to protect anyone who sought to discover them. Regi still found her story comforting all these years later. She would never forget the moment she'd seen the answer to her unspoken question reflected in her dad's sad eyes. He'd watched her scanning the other divers looking for her mom and then she'd realized the truth and felt the depth of his grief without him uttering a word. She wasn't sure why she'd felt as though she'd lost her mom again, but the deep sadness she'd seen in her dad's eyes had felt as if her world had been turned on end yet again.

She'd heard later the necklace he'd put around her neck had been uncovered when he and one of his men had moved a large piece of wreckage in their efforts to help free her. Regi looked up at Brian and commented, "The necklace my dad put around my neck when we were underwater that day was such a déjà vu moment. I glanced at it, but didn't take the time to study it until I was topside. But the surge of power I felt was so intense…I still don't even know how to describe it." She'd known by the look in her dad's eyes he'd felt the power emanating from the piece as well and it humbled her that his last act before he and his crew had been pulled into the deep was to give her the most valuable artifact he'd ever found.

The Wests' army of lawyers were negotiating the sale of that particular piece and the numbers she'd been hearing were staggering. It seemed everyone who touched the heavy piece felt the electric charge so the rumor mill was in high gear churning out tales of its capability to amplify an individual's abilities. That combined with its historic significance had sent the bidding into a frenzy.

Brian nodded, "The necklace seems to be making every newscast in the world." He laughed even as he shook his head, obviously in awe of the power of social media to light up the airways. "I understand the value in theory, but to tell you the truth I'm having trouble comprehending those numbers."

When Regi felt Brian shift her to his side, she noticed Kirk had moved up to stand along her side. Brian positioned her between the two of them, a move she knew was symbolic of the way the two men saw their relationship. Kirk gave her a knowing smile as he spoke, "I think you have to have a spiritual connection to the ancestry of the artifacts—whether it's genetic or just a deep love of the history of cultures—to understand how something can have that much value." *Leave it to Kirk to put a mystical spin on it.* She loved his deep reverence for history, he loved the land and the people of the southwest. She'd seen it in his eyes as he'd looked over the various pieces as she'd explained the stories surrounding them.

Regi also loved Brian's appreciation for the soul-centering nature of the ocean. His love of boats rivaled her dad's and she was close behind. Glancing out over the slow moving river, a large houseboat anchored near the river's arching bend caught her eye. The gentle curve in the river was almost a quarter-mile from where they were standing so she wasn't able to see the man standing on the deck as clearly as she would have liked, but everything in her stilled as the familiarity to his movements washed over her. As if he'd felt her eyes on him, the man turned and Regi would have sworn he was looking right at her.

Kirk had sensed the shift in her and she heard him asking if she was alright, but she was too transfixed to respond. Her skin felt like it was crawling when each individual hair stood on end as if she'd been jolted with electricity. *No…it can't be. He wouldn't have let me think he was gone again, would he?* Just as she decided she was letting her imagination get the best of her, she saw it…the gesture that they'd shared since she'd been a toddler. When the man on the boat pressed his fist against his chest, then slowly extended his arm and pointed toward her, Regi felt all the air leave her lungs in a rush. Everything around her narrowed to a pinpoint of light and for a couple of seconds, the only thing she could hear was the pounding of her heart before she let herself fall into the darkness.

The End

Books by Avery Gale

The Wolf Pack Series
Mated – Book One

Fated Magic – Book Two

Tempted by Darkness – Book Three

Masters of the Prairie Winds Club
Out of the Storm

Saving Grace

Jen's Journey

Bound Treasure

Punishing for Pleasure

Accidental Trifecta

Missionary Position

The ShadowDance Club
Katarina's Return – Book One

Jenna's Submission – Book Two

Rissa's Recovery – Book Three

Trace & Tori – Book Four

Reborn as Bree – Book Five

Red Clouds Dancing – Book Six

Perfect Picture – Book Seven

Club Isola

Capturing Callie – Book One
Healing Holly – Book Two
Claiming Abby – Book Three

I would love to hear from you!

Email:
avery.gale@ymail.com

Website:
www.averygalebooks.com/index.html

Facebook:
facebook.com/avery.gale.3

Instagram:
avery.gale

Twitter:
@avery_gale

Excerpt from Fated Magic

The Wolf Pack Book Two

by Avery Gale

K IT PACED THE length of her husbands' office like a caged animal during the entire meeting regarding the boy her mother simply referred to as Braden. Jameson hadn't hesitated a moment in his agreement to take the teenager in and the rest of the meeting had been taken up with logistics and planning for his safety as well as the safety of everyone else living at the estate. Kit was in favor of taking him in and knew her friend well enough to know where he'd be staying once he arrived. It was obvious that Angie had felt a very real connection to the young man and Kit was relieved that everyone was rallying around him. Her restlessness had nothing to do with Braden...no her frustration was directed entirely at her two Alpha mates.

Trying to tell me that I have to wait for the next full moon to run. Damn wolves think they can rule the world just because they are the Alphas of the pack. Don't think so, fellas, I am running tonight if I have to leap out of a damned window naked and fly into the forest on a damned broom. She'd always detested the image of witches on brooms because it was about the most ridiculous bit of imagination in history if you asked Kit. Brooms? Really? Like any self-respecting witch needed a damned broom.

Spending the past four months cooped up in the estate was taking a toll on her sanity and if she didn't get out soon she was going to be a loon. At first she'd been too busy with the babies to worry about the fact she often spent the entire day in her pajamas. But the only thing that had kept a lid on her growing frustration was the fact she'd been spending a lot of quality time in the gym expending copious amounts of energy in every sort of physical outlet she could find. Well, all but the one she wanted to be enjoying. Her husbands had, for some reason, decided vanilla sex was more acceptable for a "mother" and she was seriously considering drowning them both.

How can anyone who can be replaced by a battery-operated device consider himself the Lord and Master of his Kingdom? I didn't even get a honeymoon. Nope I went straight from caught to mated to knocked up. Once they got what they wanted all was well in the Wolf brothers little Alpha paradise. Whoever decided men should be the leaders of a pack or any other group really needed to study ancient history. Fat fairies will fly over Philly before I settle for vanilla sex for the rest of my life. It's just mean. Show me all the fun of kink and then take it away? I don't fucking think so.

She'd finally received the go-ahead from the doctors to shift and run tonight and then Jameson had "suggested" that she wait until the next full moon because of the meeting she was currently ignoring. Well she'd be showing them a thing or two in a couple of hours because she had already made arrangements for the twins to spend the night with a couple of their nannies and she planned to make an appearance in the forest come hell or spell.

www.ingramcontent.com/pod-product-compliance
Lightning Source LLC
Chambersburg PA
CBHW070852120626
46556CB00002B/956